Green

"It's not all that easy be[...], Logan told her.

"And it's not easy doing chores," she replied.

"At least you don't have people watching you all the time," he said.

"At least you don't have to shovel horse manure," she shot back.

"Really, Becca?" he asked. "Have you seen our show? Some of those lines . . ."

After half a second of shocked silence, she laughed. "You win. Come on." She held out her hand. "Let's go jump some more."

I shook my head. Figures. Another Logan groupie. Although I had to admit, he handled Becca's attitude much better than I did. I had to give him credit for that. But it didn't mean I wasn't just the slightest bit jealous.

OTHER BOOKS YOU MAY ENJOY

LIGHTS, CAMERA,
CASSIDY

episode four:
Drama

by LINDA GERBER

PUFFIN BOOKS
An Imprint of Penguin Group (USA) Inc.

PUFFIN BOOKS
Published by the Penguin Group
Penguin Young Readers Group, 345 Hudson Street, New York, New York 10014, U.S.A.
Penguin Group (Canada), 90 Eglinton Avenue East, Suite 700, Toronto, Ontario, Canada M4P 2Y3
(a division of Pearson Penguin Canada Inc.)
Penguin Books Ltd, 80 Strand, London WC2R 0RL, England
Penguin Ireland, 25 St Stephen's Green, Dublin 2, Ireland (a division of Penguin Books Ltd)
Penguin Group (Australia), 250 Camberwell Road, Camberwell, Victoria 3124, Australia
(a division of Pearson Australia Group Pty Ltd)
Penguin Books India Pvt Ltd, 11 Community Centre,
Panchsheel Park, New Delhi - 110 017, India
Penguin Group (NZ), 67 Apollo Drive, Rosedale, Auckland 0632, New Zealand
(a division of Pearson New Zealand Ltd)
Penguin Books (South Africa) (Pty) Ltd, 24 Sturdee Avenue,
Rosebank, Johannesburg 2196, South Africa

Penguin Books Ltd, Registered Offices: 80 Strand, London WC2R 0RL, England

Published by Puffin Books, a division of Penguin Young Readers Group, 2012

1 3 5 7 9 10 8 6 4 2

Copyright © Linda Gerber, 2012
All rights reserved

LIBRARY OF CONGRESS CATALOGING-IN-PUBLICATION DATA IS AVAILABLE

Puffin Books ISBN 978-0-14-241817-8

Interior designed by Theresa Evangelista
Text set in Adobe Caslon regular

Printed in the United States of America

For Mom and Dad

ACKNOWLEDGMENTS

Thanks to all the super amazing people who helped to bring this book to life: to my agent, Elaine Spencer, for cracking the whip; to my editor, Kristin Gilson, for dragging a better story out of me; to designer Theresa Evangelista for giving Cassidy covers to be proud of; to the entire Puffin sales and marketing team for getting the books onto the shelves; and to Rhett Ngawaka and June Teller for all things Aussie. Thank you!

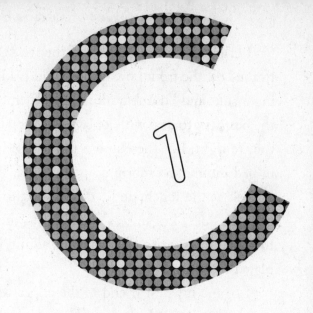

I used to think that "breathtaking" was

a lame way to describe something. "Trite" is what my tutor Victoria would say. Cliché. But my first glimpse of the Australian high country changed all that. When I slipped out the door of our rented bunkhouse to see the mountains painted rose and peach with the sunrise, I'm pretty sure I forgot to breathe.

It had been dark by the time we rolled in to the Back of Beyond ranch the night before, so I hadn't seen the mountains then. (And to be honest, after the long flight into Melbourne—over thirty hours!—the last thing I was thinking about when we got to the ranch was checking out the scenery. All I wanted to do was to take a shower and go to sleep.) But now . . .

I cringed at every squeak of the weathered boards as I tiptoed off the front porch. Mom and Dad were still sleeping inside, and I didn't want to wake them. They always say the best way to deal with jet lag is to sleep it off, and maybe they're right. But there's no way I was going to lie around in bed on my first morning in Australia. We had less than a week at the ranch, and I didn't want to miss a moment of it. Besides, Logan was supposed to meet me out front to watch the sunrise, and I have to admit, that was an even bigger draw.

Logan's my best friend in the entire world. I also happen to have a crush on him. That might be a little weird, when you consider that the two of us practically grew up together, but what can I say? I couldn't help it.

His dad is the executive producer of *When in Rome*—my mom and dad's travel show—so Logan and I both traveled around with our parents when we were little. We used to hang out while the show was filming, and we became best friends . . . until he left us to stay with his mom in Ireland for a couple of years and I never heard from him. At all.

Then, when we were filming in Spain, he returned to the show, and we picked up where we left off. Kind of. We were still friends, but things between us had changed. Mostly because I realized I liked him. I mean, really *liked* him. And that's when everything got weird.

The problem was, I didn't know if Logan liked me back. I was pretty sure he did. He was super sweet (when he wasn't teasing me). We almost kissed a couple of times. (Okay, I almost kissed him.) And he gave me a tree frog charm from Costa Rica to go on my charm necklace, which I had to take as a good sign. But I wanted to *know* he liked me, and I just didn't.

Probably because we never get to see each other for more than a week or two at a time, when we're filming a show somewhere. Did I mention that Logan and I started doing our own travel show together? Well, not really a "show," but while my mom and dad are filming *When in Rome*, Logan and I do a series of corresponding minisodes for a kids' network. Which is awesome, because it guarantees we get to spend most of our time on location together, but it also means we've got cameras following us around, so we have to be careful what we say and what we do. And then, as soon as the episodes are in the can, the show takes a break for another few weeks and everyone splits up again, and we're back to square one.

Usually, I go stay at my gramma's house in Ohio, and Logan goes back to Ireland. We text and Skype each other, but it's not the same as talking in person. It's kind of hard to get close to someone when you're oceans apart.

So I decided I was going to spend every possible minute with Logan on this trip. But so far, he wasn't cooperating. I pulled out my phone to check the time as the sun began to send pink streaks through the purple sky. Where was he? He was going to miss it!

Behind me, a neat row of small, rustic bunkhouses sat dark and silent. Since I had fallen asleep before Logan and his dad had arrived the night before, I wasn't sure which one was theirs. Not that it would have helped much if I did; I wouldn't dare go tap on his door to wake Logan up because it would probably wake Cavin—his dad—as well. Cavin wouldn't like me being up and out in the "wee hours" any more than my parents would. (I made the mistake one time of slipping out of our apartment in Spain, and it turned into a major ordeal—especially for him since he's the executive producer. Of course, he did milk it for all the publicity we could get, but still.)

I hugged my arms in the morning chill and tried to shake off the disappointment that Logan had slept in and missed our plan. Maybe it was better this way. Then he wouldn't have to see me for the first time on this trip in my pajama pants and *Wicked* T-shirt (I wore it in honor of us being in Australia. You know, they sometimes call it Oz. Never mind.) The point is, this way I could take some time getting ready. Fix my hair. Maybe even put on some lip gloss. I sighed, wandered away from the bunkhouses, and sank onto an old tree stump to watch the sun come up. Alone.

There would be other mornings—five to be exact—for Logan to watch it with me.

He might even hold my hand.

Or not.

Logan obviously wasn't as excited as I was to spend time together. Maybe he didn't like me the way I liked him.

I sighed and pushed myself up off the tree trunk, brushing the seat of my pajama bottoms to make sure I didn't have any leaves or twigs stuck to my butt.

Behind me, someone laughed. I smiled and spun around to give Logan a hug. He had woken up after all!

Only it wasn't Logan. A different boy stood in the yard, grinning at me.

"You missed a spot," he said.

Travel tip: Australians are very down

to earth and have a healthy sense of humor.

My mouth was moving. I could feel it opening and closing, but no words came out. Which is actually a good thing, because I probably wouldn't have been able to come up with anything intelligent to say. All I could think was that I was standing there in my pajamas, staring at a boy I didn't know. A very cute boy, to be exact.

"Riley Calder," he said, stretching out a hand.

Calder. Of course. His dad owned the place. Mr. Calder had come to the airport the night before to pick us up. Riley looked like him, with the same blue eyes—soft and light, like a favorite pair of faded jeans. They went really nicely with his tanned skin and the wheat-blond hair that swept across his forehead and hung just the slightest bit below his ears.

"And you are——?" he prompted.

"Oh!" I grabbed his hand and shook it. "Cassidy. Cassidy Barnett."

"Barnett," he repeated. He thought for a moment. "You the movie star, yeah?"

"Television," I corrected, and then quickly added, "but not a star! I'm just . . . on TV."

He squinted into the sunlight that was now angling down on us, and scratched at the back of his neck. "Right. On the telly. With that Irish bloke."

I kicked at the dirt. "Logan," I said.

"Yeah. You two doin' your show up here, then?"

I nodded.

"Bonza." He was smiling at me, but I couldn't help noticing that his eyes kept straying toward a couple of the big outbuildings down the hill. Like he needed to leave. Only I didn't want him to go just yet; after being stood up by Logan, it was nice to have some company. Plus, his being cute didn't hurt.

I tried to think of something to say that would convince him to hang around, but all I could come up with was, "Do you know what time it is?"

He didn't even have to check his watch. "'Bout five thirty," he said.

"Oh."

Stupid, stupid, stupid. Why couldn't anything clever ever come out of my mouth?

"Well . . ." He took a step back. "I'll see ya around."

"Oh," I said again. Jeez, now I was repeating myself. "Places to be at five thirty in the morning, huh?" Again, not so clever. I've lived on a farm, so I know chores start early when there are animals to be taken care of. But it made him stop. And smile.

"Yeah, and if I don't get there soon, Mum will be fair cheesed off, so—"

"Oy! What you doing?" A girl in boots and cutoffs stalked toward us, pulling on a pair of well-worn leather work gloves. "If you think I'm hauling feed myself, you're insane."

"Becca," Riley said to me. "My sister."

I would have guessed it, even if he hadn't told me. She had his wheat-colored hair and her eyes were the same faded-denim blue—although where his were relaxed and comfortable, hers flashed cold as they flicked over me. "Who's the sheila?"

Riley hesitated, and I guessed he had forgotten my name, so I jumped in to introduce myself. "Cassidy Barnett." Out of habit, I reached out to shake Becca's hand. She folded her arms and stared me down, so I let my hand fall to my side.

"She's with that show," Riley offered, "the one filming on the property this week."

Her left eyebrow twitched, and she gave me one last hard look before turning to Riley. "Cool story. Now come on. Let's go."

Riley shrugged apologetically. "Good meetin' ya." He turned to follow Becca.

"I could help," I said quickly, "with the chores, I mean."

Becca glanced back over her shoulder and smirked. "Oh, you will, don't worry."

Riley just smiled. "Later, Hollywood."

He jogged to catch up with his sister before I could even wave good-bye.

Hugging my arms, I watched them go. I didn't have to wonder too much what Becca meant; the Back of Beyond was Australia's version of what my dad called a "dude ranch," which back in the States is a place where city people can go to pretend they're cowboys. While we were at the Calders' ranch, the whole *When in Rome* crew would be doing the cowboy thing, Australian style. We'd also be going camping in the outback, which could qualify as a cowboy thing, I supposed. I was pretty sure I'd be doing plenty of chores in the days to come. And I could guess that if Becca had her way, they'd be the dirtiest, stinkiest chores she could find.

"Who was that?"

My stomach did a little somersault, and I turned. *Logan.*

Seeing him again after so many weeks was like drinking a cool glass of water after a long, hot hike. I started to sigh, caught myself, and turned it into a cough.

"You okay?" he asked.

I couldn't hide my smile. How cute was it that he could be concerned about me when he was barely even awake? His eyes still looked sleepy, and his bed-head hair made him look like a little boy. It was so adorable; I had to stifle another sigh. "Yeah, I'm good."

"Who were you talking to?" Logan asked again.

I told him about Riley and Becca. "They own the ranch. Or at least, their parents do."

Logan glanced down the trail, but they must have already ducked into the stables. "Why are they up so early? Why are *you* up so early?"

My smile fell away. Maybe he didn't just sleep in. Maybe he forgot he had promised to meet me. "I wanted to watch the sunrise," I said weakly. "Don't you re—"

"Hey! Morning!"

I didn't even have to look to know the voice belonged to Bayani, the show's fixer. Sure enough, when I turned around, there he was walking toward us, tugging at the hem of his shirt. His black hair was wet and combed straight back. By midmorning, it would be flopping into his eyes as usual.

"Early start?" I asked him. As the fixer, Bayani's in charge of making all the logistical arrangements for the show, like setting up locations for our shoots. Which means he usually has to check things out ahead of time.

"Always an early start," he said, giving Logan and then me a fist bump by way of greeting. "And what are you two up to, hmm?" He waggled his eyebrows, and my face instantly combusted.

"Watching the sunrise," I said, at the same time as Logan said, "Couldn't sleep."

"You'll want to get your stories straight," Bayani said, "before the parental units start asking questions." He added another eyebrow wag and danced out of the way as I took a swipe at him.

"Good thing you're up and moving anyway," he said when he was done laughing. "We're meeting at the mess hall for breakfast at seven. Don't be late or you'll be fighting for a spot at the trough. There'll be two other groups to elbow out of the way."

"Wait. We're *eating* with them?" Mom and Dad had said there would be other groups at the ranch while we were there. I just didn't know we'd be getting up close and personal with them. Not that I mind sharing the space. It just makes the whole cameras-in-your-face thing kind of awkward when there are people around to watch.

"Not exactly with them—we've got our own tables. But yeah, most of our mealtimes overlap. I could ask the concierge to sneak you in the private entrance if you're un-comfortable, though."

I started to ask him where the private entrance was before I realized he was joking.

Chuckling, Bayani walked off, no doubt feeling very clever. He left Logan and me standing uncomfortably, our conversation dead.

"Well," Logan said finally, "I guess I should—"

"Wait." I reached for his arm but stopped short of grabbing it. "Remember when we were texting last week and you said—"

"Well, here's a surprise."

What now? I turned around to find Daniel, our makeup guy, walking up the path in a pair of running pants, big dark circles of sweat under the arms of his gray T-shirt.

"What's a surprise?" Logan asked.

"You two," Daniel said, gesturing at us. "Up before the dawn. Have you not heard of beauty sleep?"

"You're up," Logan pointed out.

"Yes, but I won't have a camera trained on my face all day." Daniel turned to me. "Speaking of, you might like to try this new skin-care line I picked up at the trade show in New York. It'll help those little bumps you've got starting along your jawline. We want to head off even the threat of acne before—"

"Sounds great," I snapped, wishing the ground could just open up and swallow me whole.

Logan had the grace to change the subject. "You been working out?" He nodded toward Daniel's sweaty attire.

"Running," Daniel said. "Gotta watch the weight. Beautiful property. You should come with me tomorrow."

Logan waved him off. "No way. Only place I'm running is after a football."

That's when I lost him to the world of sports talk with Daniel. I doubt either of them even noticed when I walked away.

I think he did not know, my friend Zoe texted when I told her about how Logan stood me up that morning. **To Nikos, I must explain what I say very carefully. Boys often do not understand.**

Nikos was Zoe's boyfriend. I had managed to set them up when Nikos and I were filming a special in Greece. Sadly, I couldn't do the same for myself with Logan. We were supposed to meet to watch the sun come up, I answered. What's not to understand?

You must explain to him *why* you want to meet to watch the sun, she typed. **To you, this meeting was important. To him, he is tired, so he sleeps.**

She was right, of course. I never did tell Logan the reason I wanted us to meet. I didn't tell him that early morning was the only time we could talk alone (in theory, anyway). The rest of the time, we'd be wired with mics and the cameras would be rolling, and I wouldn't be able to tell him how much I liked him. There. I said it. Only not to him. For that, I wanted the moment to be just right. A quiet spot, a romantic sunrise. But, like I said, there would be other sunrises. I could find the perfect time.

How hard could it be?

"Are you ready, Cassie Bug?" Dad called through the bathroom door. "We should be at the mess hall by now."

I frowned at myself in the mirror and ran my hand through my very wet blonde hair. The voltage in Australia, I discovered, was too high for my little American-made blow dryer. I had used an adapter, but it still got fried. Which would make Daniel happy—he's always going on about "how natural is my friend" and he doesn't like my using blow dryers and straighteners on my hair—but it left me with dripping locks and not enough time to do anything with them. "Go on," I yelled. "I'll meet you there."

My mom and dad argued about that for a minute, but they probably knew they wouldn't win, so they gave in.

Which is how I found myself later, standing at the wide double doors of the mess hall alone, suddenly feeling very intimidated.

The place was huge. And loud. It reminded me of the middle school lunchroom at my school back in Ohio. I went there for only a couple of months, but I'll never forget that awkward moment when I walked through the door for the first time, staring at the long rows of tables, searching for a familiar face.

"Cass! Over here!"

Bayani stood by one of the back tables, waving me over. I let out the breath I'd been holding, and rushed back to where he sat with Daniel and Logan and some of the other crew members.

Cavin and Liz—the network exec in charge of Logan's and my minisodes—sat with Victoria and the rest of our team at another table. Mom and Dad stood between the two tables, shaking hands, patting backs, and checking in with the crew. It's like that whenever we come back from a break: like one big family reunion with a lot of loud catching up and telling of stories from our time away.

Liz had only just joined us in Costa Rica, so she'd never been with us after a break before and she obviously didn't get the whole reunion thing. She kept pinging her spoon against her water glass, trying to call the group to some kind of order.

"I'll go talk to her," Mom offered, and slipped away. Dad veered off to talk with Cavin.

I slid onto the bench next to Logan. He gave me a quick smile and then went back to talking with Bayani. Completely clueless. How was I ever going to tell him how much I liked him? Explain carefully, Zoe had said. I took a deep breath and tapped him on the arm. "Hey," I said in a low voice. "Can we talk? I need to tell you why I wanted—"

"Ooh, what's this? Gossip?" Daniel leaned forward onto his elbows. "Spill it. What did we miss?"

"Nothing," I said too quickly.

"Hmm." Daniel pressed his lips together and gave me a look that said we'd most definitely be talking about it later. Then he took a sip from his coffee, and his eyes strayed to the other table. "Hey, did you notice that Jack's back?" He pointed with his chin. "First time since he missed that shoot in Spain."

Logan watched the other table for a moment. "Yeah, I wondered what happened to him. Where's he been?"

"Family emergency," Daniel said. "I heard—"

"He took some personal time," Bayani cut in, emphasizing the word *personal*.

"What about the ones who came with Liz?" Logan asked, shifting gears seamlessly. "Looks like we have a whole new crew with our group this time around."

"Don't I know it." Daniel curled his upper lip like the

words had gone sour in his mouth. "See the girl?" He pointed, as if we couldn't tell which one of the crew sitting at the far table wasn't a guy. Not that we could have missed her with her pink hair. "That's Deena. She's your new makeup artist."

"Aw." Logan fake-pouted. "You mean you won't be powdering our noses for us?"

"No," Daniel sniffed. "I will not."

"Maybe you're too indispensible to the *When in Rome* group," I told him. "They can't spare you, so Liz had to bring a backup along."

"I could have done both."

Bayani leaned back in his chair, shaking his head. "How many times do I hafta tell you? With this kind of scenery, we're trying out those panoramic cameras, so we need all the hands we can get. You should be glad she brought an extra helper so you can fill in on the shoots. Good job security."

It was true. Since we travel with a small crew, almost everyone has two or three jobs to do at a given time. In Costa Rica, Daniel filled in as a boom operator. In Spain, he was our photographer. He was versatile. He didn't have to feel threatened by some girl with a makeup kit. Even though she did look kind of cool with her bright hair and even brighter smile. As I watched her, she said something to the group at the table then threw her head back and laughed, high-fiving the guy next to her. A guy I'd never seen before.

"Who's that with her?" I asked.

"New cameraman-slash-tech guy," Bayani said. "Name's Ty something or other. Want me to introduce you? He's going to be your shadow for the next week."

Bayani started to raise his arm, but Daniel pushed it back down. "Don't you dare wave them over," he hissed.

"I wasn't going to wave *them* over, just Ty." Bayani shook Daniel's hand from his arm. "What is your problem?"

"She'd come, too," Daniel said, glaring in Deena's direction. "They're like a matched set. Tweedledum and Tweedledee."

"Dude, you need to get a grip," Bayani said in a low voice. "Seriously."

Daniel sputtered, and Logan grabbed the chance to change the subject once again.

"Mmm. I smell bacon," he said. He craned his neck to watch a couple of servers in white chef aprons setting up the breakfast on an old carved-wood sideboard. "When are we going to eat?"

"Soon, I hope," Bayani said. "I'm so hungry I could eat a—"

"Don't say it," I warned him.

"—lot of bacon," he said.

Just then, Victoria tapped me on the shoulder. "Sorry

to interrupt, but your parents request that you join them. You, too, Logan."

"Aw, man," Bayani fake-whined. "You guys always get to sit at the big shots' table."

"Don't fret," Daniel told him. "I've sat there before. It's very boring."

I shot them both a dirty look, but I couldn't hide my smile as I stood up to walk to the other table. And that's when I saw a guy from one of the other groups staring right at me. I think. I wasn't going to stare back to be sure. I turned away quickly and followed Victoria. This was going to be a long week if the other guests were already gawking. Just wait until the cameras came out. Then we'd really get their attention.

Unfortunately for Victoria, she wasn't able to make her getaway quick enough after depositing Logan and me at the boring table, and she got stuck sitting with us.

"Stay," Liz invited her. "You'll want to join us for a discussion of the day's itinerary so we can determine when to fit in their school time."

As our tutor, Victoria was responsible for making sure Logan and I got three hours of schooling each day. Though honestly? Liz didn't have to worry that Victoria wouldn't be able to fit those hours into the schedule. Victoria never *stopped* teaching. I swear she could turn anything into a lesson. I was about to tell this to Liz when she shushed me.

"Quiet now. Here come our hosts."

Travel tip: English is the primary language used in Australia, but their accent and slang ("strine") may take some getting used to.

I twisted around on the bench so I could see the front door. Mr. Calder strode into the room, flanked on one side by Riley and a lady I guessed was Mrs. Calder, and on the other side by Becca and an older boy who looked so much like the others, he must have been a brother. All of them wore jeans and cowboy boots and those Australian cowboy hats with the wide brims. The sides of Becca's hat brim rolled inward. I had to admit she looked really cute.

The family also looked like a posse, striding into the dining hall like that. I was about to whisper my observation to Logan when Riley caught my eye and gave me a quick smile.

"You know him?" Logan asked.

"Met him this morning," I whispered.

"He the one you were talking to?"

"Yeah. I saw him and his—"

"G'day, all," Mr. Calder said in a booming voice. "I'm Landon Calder, and this here's my family. Welcome to our home in the Back of Beyond."

"The 'back of beyond' is another term for the bush, or the outback," Victoria whispered to Logan and me. "Clever play on words."

"I like it," I whispered back.

Liz gave us both a withering stare and looked pointedly toward Mr. Calder.

"Lots on docket today," Mr. Calder continued, "so g'head and bog in the brekkie 'cause yer gonna need yer strength."

I had no idea what he had just said, and I gave Riley a questioning look. He gestured with his head toward the breakfast laid out on the sideboard.

"I think he means we should eat," I said.

Logan practically shot out of his seat. "Good, 'cause I'm starving."

I followed Logan to the sideboard, where everyone else was just starting to line up. The man I had noticed earlier had taken a spot in the line behind us. This time he wasn't staring at me; he was fixated on my mom and dad. As they got closer to him, he quickly raised a camera and fired off a couple shots.

"Oh, great," I whispered to Logan. "A paparazzo."

"Could just be a rabid fan," he whispered back. "Probably just recognized your mum and dad."

That made sense. Especially when, after he had been bold enough to snap his pictures, several of the other tourists from the other groups grabbed their cameras as well.

Poor Mom and Dad got waylaid smiling for the fans and making nice. They even stopped to sign a few autographs. We waited for them until Mom waved us on.

"Go ahead and eat," she mouthed to me.

I continued to the sideboard, grateful that most of the other guests were older, so they probably didn't watch the kids' networks. None of them noticed me, which at that particular moment was kind of nice.

The spread looked like your typical farm breakfast—lots of food to fuel up for the work ahead. There were thick slabs of bacon, sausage, eggs, platters of fruit, a variety of cereal, and a huge basket full of rolls and sliced bread.

By the time we filled our plates and returned to the table, most of the crew was finishing up. I watched them wistfully as they escaped out the door to the green trees and sunshine. We still had a production meeting to sit through with Liz and Cavin.

"Eat quickly," Liz told us. "We have a lot to cover."

I spooned some jam on my biscuit, but I was disgusted to notice that both Logan and Victoria were spreading some kind of blackish-brown goo on theirs. Vegemite, I realized. I wrinkled my nose when the smell of it reached me.

"Ugh! How can you guys eat that stuff?"

"What?" Logan asked, taking a big bite of his biscuit. "Reminds me of Marmite, like we eat at home."

I shuddered and squeezed my eyes shut. "Please. Do *not*

talk with that stuff in your mouth. It's all over your teeth, and it looks like you've been eating—"

"Actually," Victoria cut in, "you should try it sometime, Cassidy. Vegemite and Marmite are quite good for your health. They're high in B vitamins and folic acid and are a good source of—"

Liz cleared her throat. "I hate to break up this fascinating discussion, but we do have some business to attend to. Eat. Eat."

I shoveled in my food as quickly as possible, but I still didn't finish before Liz declared it was time to start our meeting. I pushed my plate aside as she consulted her tablet computer, tapping at the screen.

"You'll be pleased to know," she announced, "that the first minisodes which aired in December earned even higher ratings than we anticipated, especially among eleven- to thirteen-year-old girls." She glanced up at Logan and didn't even bother trying to hide her doting smile. "As a result, we've had our pick of sponsors and have added several to our lineup. We'll discuss their requirements as we go along. Meanwhile, Logan, the network would like to see you become more involved in the blog. With your following—"

"The blog?" Logan asked.

"Yes, yes." Liz glanced up impatiently. "They'd like to see you contribute more to drive up readership on the blog."

I set down my fork. Contribute more? Logan didn't contribute at all. And it wasn't *the* blog, it was *my* blog. I'd started it as a sort of long-distance diary of my travels for my grampa, who was sick at the time. The network didn't even care about it until they noticed how many people were reading what I wrote. Then they offered to host the blog on the *When in Rome* site, so I could have more features, more bandwidth, and more security. I would never have accepted their help if I had known what would come of it.

When I was in Costa Rica, someone hacked into my blog, so the network added even more security protections, making it so I couldn't post directly to the blog anymore. I had to write up my entries and send them to the network and someone there would upload them. And approve them. Little by little, I was losing control of my own blog. And now they wanted to completely take it over? No way.

"Um, Liz," I began.

She held up her hand like a traffic cop. "Hold that thought. I think you'll want to hear what we have planned for you while you're in Australia." She glanced down at her tablet again. "Cassidy, the Hot Spot would like to feature you on their website to answer questions for their readers. We'll do that tonight before dinner. Later this week, the number one station in Melbourne will be sending their entertainment anchor up for an interview, which will be excellent exposure for the show. And *Teen Scene* magazine would like to feature the two of you in their Fall Fashion issue."

"Fall?" Logan asked. "It's January."

"The seasons are reversed in Australia," I told him. "Fall starts in March here."

He rolled his eyes. "I know. But it's January."

"Yes, well," Liz told him, "these types of publications are laid out months in advance. Their photographer will be up on Saturday."

And on she went. We'd be going into a town called Mansfield, would go horseback riding around the property, would learn how to work the ranch, and would even go camping in the bush. She was about to tell us more, but just then Bayani burst through the dining hall door and marched up to our table.

"Guys," he said, "we've got a problem."

"We went to go get set up for the outdoors shoot," he explained to Liz, "and when we got to the storage room, we found it flooded. We've got boxes of equipment in there, half of it ruined. We're talking computers, prompters, connector cables, the whole nine yards."

Cavin deserted Mom and Dad and crossed to our end of the table. "Flooded? Whatd'ye mean, flooded?"

Bayani shot him a look that could curdle Vegemite. "I mean water," he said. "Lots of it. Running down the wall and all over the boxes. Check out this list." He shoved a clipboard into Cavin's hands. "All of it ruined."

"Oy, what's all the shemozzle?" Mr. Calder pushed out through the kitchen's swinging doors, wiping his hands on a dish towel.

Cavin and Bayani explained about the flooded storage room and the ruined equipment.

Suddenly, Mr. Calder dropped his swagger and, strangely, a bit of his Australian accent. "I can assure you," he said in a low voice, "this sort of thing has never happened before. I can't imagine how—"

"Perhaps a leak," Mom said. "A burst pipe?"

"Let's go have a look," Dad suggested.

"Good oil." Mr. Calder eyed the curious looks of the remaining diners and added, "We'll cover any damages, of course."

"Of course," Cavin agreed.

"The important thing," Liz said, "is that we are able to stick to the shooting schedule. We will be able to stick to the schedule, won't we?"

Bayani looked at her like her hair had turned green. "Half of our equipment is *ruined,*" he said. "Without it, we can shoot only one group at a time."

Cavin shook his head. "No good. We have only the one week to get everything in the can."

"Well, that's it, then," Dad said. "We'll have to find a place to rent replacement equipment, like we did when the airline lost our baggage in Spain."

"No time," Bayani said. "Takes three hours to get to Melbourne and three hours to come back, plus the time it takes to hunt down what we need. There's a whole day wasted."

Mr. Calder scratched the back of his neck—just like

Riley had done that morning. "Why don'cha try Mans-field? I know it ain't the big smoke like Melbourne, but it's no woop woop, either. Good chance they'll have whatever you're looking for."

"It's worth a shot," Dad said.

"Let's all go," Liz suggested brightly. "We planned to visit Mansfield on Thursday, anyway. Why not mix it up a little? We can shoot both groups together, and I'm sure Bayani can make arrangements to switch the restaurant visit to this afternoon."

"It's not that simple," Bayani said.

"Then I suggest you simplify it." The charm leeched from Liz's voice. "We do not have days or even hours to waste. There's no sense in making two trips into town when we can simply change the outing to today."

"It does make sense to consolidate," Mom agreed, "if it would work."

"We'll make it work," Cavin said. "How soon can we get rolling?"

Mr. Calder draped his dish towel over the back of a chair. "Straightaway. Give me a moment to check on that room, then I'll bring the fourbies 'round and we're off like a bucket of prawns."

Cavin pulled out his cell phone. "We'd better rouse the troops." Liz was already barking orders into hers.

"I need to run back to my room to grab my phone," I said to no one in particular.

Liz glanced over at me and covered her receiver with her hand. "Quick wardrobe change while you're at it," she said. "You'll find a bag of clothing I dropped by your room last night. Try the striped T-shirt with the ruffles and the cuffed denim shorts."

I looked down at the outfit I had carefully chosen that morning. "What's wrong with what I'm wea—"

"Sponsors, Cassidy," she said sharply. "Let's keep them happy, shall we?" She waved me off and turned back to her phone call before I could protest again.

What choice did I have? I stalked out of the mess hall grumbling to myself. Liz told me once that the reason the sponsors wanted to dress me up like a paper doll was because I was "known" for my "unique sense of style," which basically means my picture often turned up in tabloids or fan magazines with some comments about what I was wearing. In Spain, it had earned me the nickname *la chica moda*—the fashionable girl. I don't know how true that was, but the name kind of stuck. The thing was, if other people kept choosing clothes for me to wear, then my style stopped being all that unique, didn't it?

That's what I should have said to Liz. I should have told her I'd look at the clothes the sponsors had sent, and *if* I liked them, I might consider wearing them. I wanted to be free to make my own decisions about—

"G'day."

I caught my breath and jumped back a step. I'd been so

focused on Liz and the wardrobe mandate that I almost ran smack into Riley. "G'day," I said back to him.

"Ooh, almost. It's more like 'gidday,'" he corrected.

"Gidday," I said.

"Hmm. Needs a little practice."

"I'll work on it."

He hooked his thumbs around his belt loops, rocked back on his heels, and laughed. "You do that."

"You're all cowboyed up," I observed. He'd been wearing a T-shirt and jeans and no hat when I'd seen him that morning, but when he came into the dining hall with his family, he'd added a blue-and-green gingham shirt, his Australian cowboy hat, and boots. Not that I was fixated on what he was wearing or anything.

"Jackarooed," he told me, "not cowboyed." When I made a confused noise, he explained. "In these parts, station hands are called jackaroos, not cowboys. Or jillaroos, if they're girls. When we have guests at the ranch, Mum and Dad want us to dress the part. They say tourists like that kind of stuff."

"I understand." And I really did. Understand, I mean. Riley had to dress up and pretend, just like me. "Well, you can relax around my group, anyway. We're going on a little road trip today, so we won't be around to be impressed."

He pushed his hat back on his head and grinned. "Oh, so you're impressed?"

It was my turn to laugh. "Nice try."

"Where you going?" he asked.

"Mansfield," I told him, "to get some shots around town, and then—"

"Riley! Oy!" Riley's brother yelled up the trail. "Group two. Sheep corral. Move it!"

"Duty calls," Riley said. He gave me an exaggerated tilt of his hat and a cheesy smile. "Hoo roo, Hollywood."

"Hoo roo," I called. Then he was gone.

The jeeps were idling in front of the dining hall when I returned. I had changed into the striped T-shirt like Liz asked me to, but instead of the cuffed shorts, I chose a pair of my own cutoff jeans and threaded one of the sponsor-gifted scarves through the belt loops to tie around my hips. I'd found a pair of white-rimmed sunglasses in the bag and stuck those on top of my head to complete the look. If Liz didn't like it, she could go jump with the kangaroos and wallabies.

But Liz hardly even noticed. She was too busy barking orders at the new crew to give me more than a glance. "Get her wired," she told Ty. "We're running behind."

Some of the other guests stood around in clusters, watching the spectacle. Most of them just gawked politely, but I noticed the guy from the mess hall, walking around the front jeep, brazenly snapping off photos.

I nudged Logan. "It's the camera guy," I said, pointing with my chin. "You think he's with the tabloids?"

Logan laughed. "With that camera?" He had a point. It was a little aim-and-shoot. Didn't even look as if it had a zoom. "And check out the black socks with the sandals. Tourist."

"Annoying tourist," I said, as Ty called us over.

Ty hooked me up to the lav mic while Deena finished up with Logan. A lav mic is the little clippy mic you can sometimes see on a person's lapel or shirt collar. It's wired to a transmitter you can slip into your pocket or clip to your belt, or, in my case, since it needed to stay hidden, tape to your skin under your clothes. The thing I hate about lav mics (besides the uncomfortable transmitter) is that once you're "wired," you have to be careful what you say because the mic will pick up every word.

Logan met my eye and mouthed, "Here we go."

I pantomimed cheering. Sarcastically. Because even though I loved that I got to do a "reality" show with Logan, I hated that we couldn't truly talk to each other while doing it.

"All right," Liz told Logan and me, "we have just over an hour's drive to get to Mansfield. I've asked Victoria to ride with you so we can save time by getting part of your lessons out of the way while in transit."

I gave Victoria a questioning look, and she shrugged helplessly. Once Liz had made up her mind, there was no discussion.

"Deena will attend to your makeup," Liz continued,

"and Ty will man the camera. You five will be in jeep number three. Any questions?"

As if any of us would dare ask a thing.

Mr. Calder walked up just then with Riley's brother and an older gentleman, all in boots and Australian-style cowboy hats. "I'd like you all to meet son Ryan, and my most trusted man, Malo," Mr. Calder said. "He'll be your driver today."

"G'day," Malo said, tipping his hat to us. He stood several inches shorter than Mr. Calder, with a wide face, laughing black eyes, and dark skin that contrasted with his wiry white hair. "Let's get you loaded up, and off we go, right?"

We climbed into our jeep as Ryan and Mr. Calder went off to load up the other two. I settled onto the second seat with Logan on one side of me and Deena and her makeup kit on the other. Ty set up in the far back seat so he could record the drive for posterity. This left Victoria riding shotgun with Malo.

A few miles down the road, Victoria twisted around as much as her seat belt would allow so she could try to get in those lessons Liz talked about, but it didn't work very well. It was kind of hard to hear her from up front, and she had to stop what she was saying every time Deena interrupted to give Logan or me directions.

"Turn your head." "Look up." "Flip your hair back." "Lips open, like this. Ehhhh."

After each disruption, Victoria tried to pick up where

she'd left off, but I'll admit that neither one of us was really listening. It's hard enough to pay attention in a classroom setting with our books in front of us. Throw in a camera pointed at you and a mascara wand coming at your eye in a moving car, and concentrating is next to impossible.

Victoria's voice kept rising, along with her frustration. Which made Deena talk louder while she told us what to do. Which made Ty complain about feedback in the mics. Which made Logan and me tune out even more.

Malo had been watching the whole thing silently through the rearview mirror, but when Victoria paused for a breath, he asked, "May I?"

She blinked at him for a second, then settled back into her seat. "Be my guest."

He slowed the jeep and pointed off to the side of the road. "This here's the trail," he said softly, "of the notorious Ned Kelly."

With the hum of the car in my ears, I could barely hear what he said. I leaned forward in my seat. "Ned who?"

"Ned Kelly, the bushranger," Malo told me. "Or the hero. Depending on who ya ask."

Logan leaned in closer to me. "What's a bushranger?"

"The bushranger is an outlaw," Malo explained, "a bloke who hides out in the bush whilst doing his deeds. This Ned Kelly had his run-in with the law, but it weren't until the ambush at Stringy Bark Creek that he became an outlaw."

Even Deena was listening now. She paused with her

foundation brush in midair and asked, "What kind of ambush?"

"Four lawmen," Malo said, "came out here to the Wombat Ranges to find the hiding place of Ned Kelly and his gang. Three of them were killed just few kilometers from here."

I shuddered. "What happened?"

"Shoot-out," Malo said. "It was the beginning of the end for Ned Kelly."

"Wait," Deena said, suddenly animated. "I know this story. Heath Ledger, right?"

"What are you talking about?" Ty asked.

"Heath Ledger was Ned Kelly!" She might have bounced out of her seat if it weren't for the seat belt. "He was an Irish Australian dude, and he went on the run because of some false charges by this lame constable, and he made his own armor and protested against the government and became like this big folk hero."

"Who murdered three policemen," Ty reminded her.

"That totally wasn't his fault," she protested. "He just wanted the cops at the creek to surrender, right, Malo?"

"There is always more than one side to every story," Malo said. "Who is to say what happened?"

Deena shook her head. "I just can't believe Heath Ledger would play a murderer."

"Um, hello?" Ty said. "Did you ever see him in *Batman*? His Joker character was seriously disturbed."

"You said we were on a trail," I said to Malo. "Where does the trail go?"

"Through Mansfield," he said. "You'll see heaps plenty of Ned Kelly memos in town. Including a memorial dedicated to them policemen."

"Who wouldn't have gotten killed if they had just surrendered," Deena added.

"If there are so many sides of one story," I asked, "how can you ever know what the truth is?"

Malo thought for a moment. "When the British ruled Australia, many of my ancestors served as trackers because they could find people and places in the bush the English could not. The tracker would walk around and around until he could see what was hidden. The truth is sometimes a hidden thing, I think. You must be willing to keep walking to find it."

C5

Our convoy of jeeps attracted some attention when we pulled into Mansfield. A few curious passersby peered at the tinted windows, but they didn't stop and stare or anything like that . . . until we all climbed out and the cameramen started setting up equipment. Then you'd think we were neon-purple aliens or something. It didn't take long for a crowd to gather.

"Cassidy," Liz said in a low voice, "try not to look quite so intimidated. We do need usable footage from this excursion."

"I don't look intimidated," I grumbled under my breath.

Liz lowered her earpiece. "Yes, you do." Stupid lav mics. "Now ignore the spectators and concentrate on having a good time. Smile."

"I am smiling."

"Like you mean it."

I turned to Logan and flashed him an exaggerated, mugging grin. He laughed, but it only made Liz correct me again.

"Toward the camera!" she said. "Always face the camera!"

Bayani went off with Mr. Calder to find a place to rent equipment, so Malo and Ryan offered to show us around town. In a couple of hours, Mom and Dad were scheduled to do a segment at a local restaurant that specialized in regional cuisine, but until then we would sightsee as a group until Bayani was able to locate more equipment so we could film some B roll.

As we walked down the main drag, I could practically feel the weight of everyone's stares following us. I can't be sure, but I think most people on the street were tourists, judging by the cameras they kept pointing in our direction (and the number of unfortunate socks-with-sandals combinations Logan and I counted). Which made sense, since Mansfield was sort of a tourist town. It's in a resort area with a lot of gift shops and cafés and storefronts advertising day trips to the mountains or the bush, or to the ski slopes in the winter.

"What do you think of the public art?" Victoria asked, pointing out a tall pole with skis lashed to it. "Don't you think it gives the town character?"

"What is it?" I asked.

Logan laughed. "It's a ski pole. Get it? A pole with skis?"

Okay, so different people had different ideas about what was art. I was more interested in the silhouette cutout on the other side of the pole, of a jackaroo riding a horse in full stride.

"That's the Man from Snowy River," Ryan told us.

"Oh! I saw that," Deena said. "Old movie, right? I loved the piano music in that one. Was it filmed around here?"

"It was," Ryan said proudly. "This here's Snowy River country."

"Do they still have those wild horses—what were they called . . . brumbies?—out there in the mountains?" she asked.

"We got brumbies come onto the property pretty often," he told her. "We'll be going out to scout for them this afternoon to see if we can't muster 'em up, if you want to ride along."

I thought Deena would swoon. "Get out! That would be awesome!"

At almost the same moment, someone behind me matched Deena's tone exactly. "Oh. My. Gosh," the girl said. "Look, Maggie! Is that who I think it is?"

I snuck a quick peek over my shoulder. A couple of girls about my age were staring right at me. I ducked my head to hide my smile. I'd gotten used to being recognized, especially after the tabloids branded me *la chica moda*. It wasn't so fun when it was the paparazzi that singled me out, but these girls probably just wanted a picture or something. I pasted a benevolent smile on my face and started to turn toward them when the shorter one shrieked into her cell phone. "Dinky-di! I'm telling you, it's that boy from the telly! Yes. At High Street and Collopy! Hurry!"

My smile fell away. So it wasn't me they were excited to see. It was Logan. Of course.

He stood next to me, pretending not to hear, but it was obvious by his crooked grin and the way he squared his shoulders that he was completely aware of the commotion behind him. He noticed my watching and his smile only got wider. "What d'ya think? Should I wave at 'em?"

"Oh, absolutely," I said drily. "Give them a thrill."

The dope actually thought I was serious. He turned around and gave each one of the girls one of his patented chin-jerk greetings and a little flutter of his fingers. And wouldn't you know, they *were* thrilled. The short one squealed (my ears are still recovering), and the other one giggled, which I guess I can understand because Logan looked so ridiculous trying to be suave. I might have giggled myself if I hadn't been so annoyed.

I mean, it was cool that Logan had fans and everything, but a tiny part of me resented the fact that he was the one getting all the attention when no one would even have known who Logan was if it weren't for me. If I hadn't suggested to the network that Logan do the minisodes with me, these girls might have stopped to stare at him for a moment (because, seriously, he is that cute), but they wouldn't be calling every other girl in town to tell them about the sighting.

"Hmm," Liz said as she watched the spectacle. Then she whipped out her phone and paced away from the group. I figured she was calling for some security or something, the way she kept looking over at us and waving her free hand around as she spoke.

It wasn't long after that Bayani and Mr. Calder pulled up in one of the jeeps and threw open the back to unload a couple more cameras and a trolley. "Got here as fast as we could," he assured Liz.

"Fine, fine," she said, as she herded Ty over to the cameras. "You have everything you need?" she asked him.

He hefted one of the cameras and settled it onto his shoulder. "She's an older model," he said, "but she'll do."

"Perfect." She stood back and smiled as if she were the one who had hunted down the extra equipment. "It's all set then."

"What's all set?" I asked, but she didn't seem to hear me. She turned to Bayani instead.

"We'll be fine," she told him. "You may go set up for the restaurant segment."

By the time Mom and Dad's group split off, a whole gaggle of girls were trailing behind us.

"There are so many of them," Victoria said wonderingly.

Liz just smiled. "Oh, the show is quite popular in the Australian market."

"But it's not that big of a town," I pointed out.

Again, Liz seemed not to hear me. She was too busy directing Ty how to keep Logan in the shot, while at the same time capturing his hordes of adoring fans. Finally, I just gave up.

"Come on," I told Victoria. "Let's see what else there is to do around here."

Ryan continued our tour of the town, and the growing cluster of girls followed. (Seriously, where were they all coming from?)

At first they tried to be sly about watching us, pretending they were studying shop windows, or that they were taking pictures of one another when clearly they had their cell phones pointed directly at Logan. But as the group grew, they started to get bolder, edging closer to our group, openly following us, and even calling Logan's name. It was starting to get annoying.

And not just to us.

Several people sitting on the benches in the park or eating at outdoor restaurant tables got up to leave. Some of the locals shot us disapproving looks. Especially when our unwanted entourage became more vocal. And emotional. Several hyperventilating girls pushed their way to the front of the crowd, squealing, crying, begging for Logan to notice them.

"Oh, my gosh," I said to Victoria. "Logan has groupies."

She could barely hide her smile. "Yes. It would appear he does."

Liz clapped her hands. "Brilliant!" Then, to Ty, "Make sure you get this."

Ty motioned for Victoria and me to get out of the way, and I stepped back even though I felt like jumping in front of the camera to save Logan the embarrassment of living through the spectacle more than once.

Except . . .

Logan didn't seem to be bothered by it at all. In fact, he flashed his lopsided Irish smile and waved to them. Which only produced more scream-squeals. And when a couple of the braver girls approached Logan, begging for his autograph, he didn't even hesitate but whipped out a pen (since when did he carry a pen?) and signed whatever they could find for him. I turned away when one girl asked if he could sign her T-shirt.

"He said he didn't like playing to the camera," I grumbled, "but look at him."

Victoria's smile faded. "Pardon?"

"Nothing."

When Liz decided she had enough autograph footage, she shooed the girls back to the gathering of groupies. Logan did the aw-shucks routine when he came over to stand by Victoria and me, suddenly humble and shy. "How do you get used to people asking for your autograph?" he asked me.

"I don't," I told him. Mainly because people don't usually *ask* for my autograph. But I wasn't going to tell him that.

"You handled it well, Logan," Liz praised. "It's important to maintain the image of someone who is friendly, yet not-quite-attainable."

I snorted at that and waited for Logan to deliver some kind of zinging wisecrack about being unattainable, but he lapped up her words like she was some Zen master sharing the wisdom of the ancients.

"I think I'm going to be sick," I muttered.

"What was that?" Liz tore her attention away from Wonder Boy long enough to glance over at me.

"We should move along quick," I said. "Before the mob overtakes us."

"Quickly," Victoria corrected.

"Yeah," I agreed. "That."

We paraded around town with our following of fangirls for what felt like way too long. Finally, even Liz had to admit that the entourage had become a nuisance. They were noisy. They kept getting in the way and spoiling our shots. She was no longer pleased by their presence and proclaimed that we should move uptown, away from them.

But our trying to escape only made the girls more determined to follow. They started shoving each other, trying to get to the front of the pack . . . which was beginning to get uncomfortably close.

"I don't like this," Ty said. "The natives are getting restless."

Liz frowned and nodded in agreement. "Is there someplace we could go," she asked Ryan, "until they disperse?"

He squinted up at the sun. "Well, I s'pose it's about lunchtime. We could drop into a milk bar and grab a feed."

"A milk bar?" I laughed. "Like, they serve you milk?"

Ryan pushed his hat back and scratched his head like he didn't understand my question. "They can serve milk, if you want it."

"So it's a bar, and it serves milk." I wasn't trying to be dense, but it painted such a funny picture in my head. I could imagine one of those scenes from an old Western, where a cowboy sidles up to the bar and says, "Give me a cold one!" and instead of sarsaparilla or beer, the bartender slides a frosty mug of two-percent down the counter to him.

"Yesss," he said slowly. "Or you could get juice, or lolly water. Even a sanger if you fancy a counter lunch."

"And groceries, yes?" Victoria asked. "Newspapers? Magazines?" When Ryan nodded, she explained to me, "We have milk bars in the U.K. as well. They're like general stores with a lunch counter. And they often sell milk shakes."

"Ooh." Now the name made sense. And it did sound good. "I'm up for it."

"Me, too," Logan agreed.

Liz eyed the rabid fans behind us. "Where's the closest one?"

Ryan led us to a shop down the the street and held the

door open for us as we ducked inside. Ty blocked the entrance while Ryan had a quick word with the guy behind the register. I'm guessing they were friends, judging by the casual way Register Guy greeted Ryan. Also because he kept laughing as Ryan pointed over at us. I would like to have known what he said. The guy came out from behind the counter to shoo a couple of kids away from the comic books and out the door, and then turned the sign on the door around so that it said CLOSED.

"All right," he said. "I can give you half an hour. My manager will have my hide if I lock the doors much longer than that."

"We appreciate it," Liz said.

"No worries."

Liz walked farther into the store, the wood-plank floor creaking beneath her feet. "Your establishment is charming. May we have your permission to film in here?"

Register Guy exchanged a look with Ryan, and shrugged. "I s'pose."

She pulled a folder out of her bag. "We'll just need you to sign this release . . ."

Register Guy passed out water and soda (or lolly water, as Ryan called it) and set to work making poached chicken sandwiches for the whole group.

"They're not going away." Deena pointed toward the store's front window, where at least three girls were peering inside with hands cupped around their eyes, their faces smashed up against the glass. A bunch of other girls crowded around them. From where we sat, they all looked like one big mass of rabid fandom.

Liz scowled. "Their devotion is not cute anymore."

"It never was cute," I said.

Logan bumped my arm with his. "You're just jealous."

Jealous? That was ridiculous. But still, it stung. "Oh, right. I'm green with envy."

"Don't feel bad," he said. "I'm sure you'd have a horde of fans following you, too, except"—he gestured with his head toward the window—"guys aren't that aggressive."

"Really." I crossed my arms. "You ever been to a football game? 'Cause I'm pretty sure guys are *way* more aggressive than girls."

"Yeah, but we're not, like, 'Oh, she's so cute!'" He made his voice go falsetto when he said that, and I couldn't help but laugh. Until he added, "Besides, you don't see any guys out there chasing us down, do you?"

No, I didn't. "So?" I said. Great comeback. "I'm not limited to having fans who are guys. In fact, my fan clubs are mostly girls. Girls like me. Girls want to be like me."

"Okay. Whatever you say." He shrugged and went back to eating his sandwich.

Which made me mad, because I knew what he wasn't saying. I might have little pockets of fans here and there. A lot of them might be girls. But *this* group didn't care who I was. No one was following *me* around.

I set my sandwich down. Suddenly, I wasn't hungry anymore.

"I believe," Victoria said, "we've had enough filming for this afternoon."

Liz narrowed her eyes at Logan and me for a moment, but then she nodded. "Yes. I think you may be right. We can pick back up at the property this evening."

"What do we do here in the meantime?" Ty asked. He

pointed to the girls. "We can't go out there again. We'll get mobbed."

"Sorry, mate," Register Guy said, "but you can't stay here, either. I gotta open back up."

Liz nodded slowly again, then slid from her barstool and clapped her hands. "Right. Then we'll return to the ranch. The other group can meet us when they've finished filming. Now"—she turned to Register Guy—"is there a back exit?"

For half a second he hesitated, but then he wisely realized Liz was not going to take no for an answer. He sighed and pushed open a swinging door behind the counter. "Right then," he said. "Come with me."

Everyone started filing into the stock room. I followed behind Logan, and then almost bumped into him when he stopped to look back at the girls at the window.

"Don't worry," I told him. "They're still there."

"Who's worried?"

I was. But I wasn't going to tell him that.

We didn't even try to slip in a lesson on the ride back to the ranch. Victoria probably sensed that I really wasn't in the mood. I caught her a few times, peeking back to look at me. I saw the questions on her face. Finally, I just closed my eyes and pretended to be asleep.

I didn't really want to talk to anyone right then anyway. Maybe Logan was right. Maybe I was jealous. Not just because he had more fans than me, either. Those other girls, they *liked* him, and it made me feel panicky and protective.

How was I supposed to explain that to Logan?

Mrs. Calder met the jeep as it pulled into the courtyard. "Heard you ran into a bit of a snag in town."

Victoria waved away the worry. "It was simply a few overenthusiastic young ladies."

I snorted. "Ladies?"

"Shame you had to cut your day short," Mrs. Calder said.

"Well, I don't mind." Deena climbed out of the backseat. "I could do with a power nap before the rest of the crew gets back."

Ty poked her. "Wimp."

"Whatever. I need my beauty sleep." She stretched her arms over her head and yawned. "Later."

Victoria hid her own yawn behind her hand. "Goodness. That certainly is contagious."

"You should get some rest, too," Mrs. Calder said. "You look plain knackered."

"We still have some lesson time to get through," Victoria said, yawning again.

"Rubbish." Mrs. Calder took Victoria by the shoulders and turned her around so that she was facing her bunkhouse. "Becks and Riley can keep this lot occupied. You go get some kip."

"But—"

"Now, don't fret yer freckle," Mrs. Calder said, giving her a gentle shove. "I won't let your young charges get eaten by the crocs or the dingoes."

Victoria looked at Logan and me over her shoulder "We'll have some review time tonight," she promised.

Logan gave her the thumbs-up, and I said, "Can't wait!" but I think she was too far gone to even pick up on the sarcasm. She just nodded and then stumbled off toward her room.

"Ah, there you are," Mrs. Calder said, looking beyond where Logan and I stood. "I was just about to call you."

Travel tip: Often mistaken for being rude and lacking in tact and diplomacy, Australians can be rather blunt.

Riley and Becca were just coming out of the main house in shorts and flip-flops. Riley was wearing a plain white T-shirt with big holes ripped in it, and Becca had on her cutoffs and a swim-suit top. She took one look at Logan and me and stopped dead where she stood.

"Oh, good," Mrs. Calder said. "Riley and Rebecca. Just who I was looking for."

"Riley and me are headed for the creek," Becca said flatly.

Mrs. Calder clapped her hands. "Corker of an idea." And then to Logan and me she asked, "Did you two bring your bathers?"

"Bathers?" I asked.

"Togs. Cossies." Mrs. Calder continued.

"Swimsuits," Riley translated. "We're going to swim in the creek, if you want to come."

Logan said yes, but I wasn't so sure. Becca's frown and tightly folded arms weren't exactly an open invitation.

"We don't want to crash your plans," I said.

Logan shot me a look. "Sure we do."

"Ace." Riley elbowed Becca before she could protest. "We'll wait for you."

After Logan and I had changed, we met Riley and Becca at the garage, which actually looked like a barn. You wouldn't know it was a garage from the outside, but inside, there were parking spaces for jeeps instead of stalls for cows or horses. It smelled like a garage, too, a sharp mix of rubber, grease, and motor oil. A rack of tools hung on the wall, and a stack of tires stood neatly in one corner.

In the other corner, Becca pulled back a tarp to reveal a couple of four-wheel ATVs.

"Are we going to ride those?" I asked. It was a perfectly legitimate question, but Becca rolled her eyes as she folded up the tarp.

"Unless you want to walk," she snarked.

Riley was a little more gentle. "The creek's pretty far out," he said. "We usually take these. Long as we stay on the property, we're okay."

Logan ran his hand along the black-gripped handlebars. "They're wicked sick."

Becca thawed a little as she gave him half a smile. "Thanks." You'd think she was personally responsible for creating the things.

"Hope you don't mind doubling up," Riley said. "Dad only lets us use the two."

Logan wagged his head, still petting the handlebars. "No worries from me."

Becca brushed his hand away as she climbed onto the seat and pulled on her helmet, but she tossed another helmet to him and said, "You ride with me." He scrambled on behind her as the engine roared to life.

Riley handed me a helmet almost apologetically. "Looks like you're stuck with me," he shouted.

"Good," I told him. "I was hoping I would be." What I meant was that I didn't want to ride with prickly Rebecca, but I think Riley may have taken it to mean something else because his face went red and he ducked his head away from me as he slipped on his helmet. "Oh. I mean . . ."

But then I saw his smile. And I decided not to explain.

I climbed onto the seat behind Riley as he started the engine. The vibration of it rumbled in my stomach and made my skin itch. But I didn't have much time to think about that, because the very next moment, we were off, racing behind Becca and Logan out of the garage.

Clouds of red dust billowed up behind the ATVs as

we bounced over the fields and raced past clumps of scrub brush. I closed my eyes and let the hot wind wash over my face, loving the freedom. Out there in the dirt, there were no cameras, no lav mics, no network. And no hordes of screaming girls. Now if I could just figure out what Rebecca's problem was, we'd be set.

The creek snaked lazily through a low-lying corner of the property. It was maybe as wide as a two-lane street, the path carved deep in the dirt and rock. We rolled to a stop near an extra-wide spot, where the creek curved around a rocky outcrop. From out of the rocks grew a gnarled tree that bent right over the edge. The setup looked like a picture postcard, almost too perfect to be real.

Becca pulled off her helmet and hung it on one end of the handlebars. She pointed to the rocks and told Logan, "Come on, then. I'll show you how it's done."

"How what's done?" I asked, but she was already at the water's edge, pulling her shirt off over her head. Riley and Logan were close behind. I hurried after them. "What are we going to do?" I asked again.

Riley grinned. "You'll see."

We laid our shirts and shorts on some of the bigger rocks and waded into the cool water in our sandals and bathers, as Mrs. Calder called them. The streambed dropped off quickly, so the water was nearly chest high before we were halfway across.

"It's even deeper over there," Riley told me, pointing. That's where we'll jump."

That's when I saw the rope swing hanging from the tree. "Oh, my gosh," I breathed. "That is so cool."

Riley gave me a weird look. "It's just a rope swing."

"You don't understand," I said, pushing through the water as fast as it would let me. "I've only seen rope swings like that in movies and books. I've never actually been on one."

"It's just a rope," he said again. "On a tree."

"I know," I gushed. "It's perfect." I didn't know how to explain it to him. I'd been all over the world. I'd gone bungee jumping off a bridge in Nepal, and zip-lining in the cloud forests in Costa Rica, but I had never swung on a rope and jumped into a creek in my own country. It was such a normal summer kid thing to do—at least it seemed so to me. And it was just one more normal thing I never got to experience. Until now.

We climbed up the back side of the rock to reach the tree. Riley pulled the rope in and held the end out to me. "Since you're so excited, you can go first."

I took a step back. Now that we were on top of the rock, it looked like a long way down. Besides, since I'd never done it before, I didn't know the technique. "I think I'd like to watch you guys do it first."

"Give it to me." Becca grabbed the rope from Riley and shot me a look that said I was possibly the lamest person she'd ever met. Then, with a *woop!* she ran straight for the edge of the rock and jumped. The rope creaked on the branch above our heads as she swung out, out, out, and then, as the pendulum began to swing the other way, Becca let go of the rope and dropped with a splash into the water below.

Riley pulled the rope back to where we stood on the rock, and offered it to me again. "See? Nothing to it. You wanna give it a burl?"

I might have stalled if it wasn't for that look from Becca. No way was I going to give her the satisfaction of thinking I couldn't do it. I took the rope.

"Hold it here," Riley said, showing me. "Run and jump. Simple. Just don't forget to let go."

I laughed, but at the same time, I could seriously see myself still holding on to the rope and slamming into the side of the rock on the return swing. "Run, jump, let go of the rope," I said, giving him a thumbs-up. "Got it."

He stepped back, and I was on my own. Taking a deep breath, I strangled the rope and ran four steps to the edge. Right at the last moment, I closed my eyes so I wouldn't chicken out . . . and jumped.

The first second or so was a free fall. My stomach flipped as I went down, and then again as the rope snapped tight and I swung out and over the water. It lifted me up, up, my stomach still tumbling. Blue sky above, water below, me twisting, turning, breathless. And then I was falling again. I let go of the rope and dropped into the creek with a splash. Cool water closed over my head.

I shot to the surface laughing. "That was awesome!"

Becca stood on one of the smaller rocks that lined the edge of the creek bed. "Ripper," she said. "Now get out of the way."

"Huh?"

She pointed up to where Riley and Logan stood by the tree, as if they were waiting for me to move so they could jump, but Riley was still pulling in the rope. Rebecca's attitude was getting old really fast. It's not like I was holding anyone up or anything. I swam quickly to the side anyway. Sometimes it just doesn't pay to argue.

We took turns jumping from the rope for at least an hour before Rebecca plopped down on one of the rocks and turned her face to the sun, apparently a signal that we were taking a break. I would have liked to keep going, but again, I wasn't going to say anything. Why give her anything else to snipe about?

Besides, I have to admit, after all that climbing and swimming, it felt good to sit for a while. I didn't realize how worn-out I was until I settled down next to her and my muscles practically melted.

I leaned back, propped up on my elbows, the rock warm beneath my skin. "I could get used to this," I said.

Becca snorted (not attractive) and shot a meaningful look at Riley. What kind of meaning, I didn't know, but it for sure wasn't nice.

"What?" I demanded. I know, I said it wasn't worth picking a fight, but enough is enough.

Becca blinked at me innocently. "What, what?"

"Cass . . ." Logan gave me a tiny shake of the head.

I ignored him. "You have a problem with me?"

"Why would I have a problem?"

"That's what I'd like to know."

"Who wants to go again?" Riley started to get up, but Becca stopped him with a glare. He settled back onto his rock, fidgeting with the frayed hem of his shorts.

"This sort of thing?" Becca made a big circle with her finger to take in the rock, the tree, and the creek. "The time out to do this is something my brother and I have to work for. While you were getting your pampered-princess beauty sleep, we were up getting our chores done so we'd have some time for ourselves."

"Um, Becca," Riley cut in, "she was up early, too. I talked with her on the way to the stables."

She gave him an icy stare to shut him up. "The point is, here she's saying she could *get used to this,* when all she has to do is lounge around all day."

"Actually, we were working, too," Logan said.

Her face softened when she turned to him. "I'm sure

you were." Oh, brother. "But then you get to come back and play, whereas we had to earn it."

I bristled. Earn it? "At least you have time to get away by yourself. We always have a camera pointed at us."

She threw up her hands in mock horror. "Oh, how terrible!"

"Don't listen to her," Riley told me, "she's just jealous."

"Of course I'm jealous," Becca snapped. "Sure would be nice to get whatever you want, whenever you want it."

"Yes, it would," I agreed, "but that's not how it is."

She folded her arms. "Oh, right. Yet you had three deliveries just today. Who do you think had to unpack your designer togs?"

"Those designer *togs*," I told her, "are nothing I want. They're from our sponsors. I never asked for them. How would you like being dressed up like some corporate doll?"

"In those clothes? I think I *could get used to it*."

"Clever," I said.

She flipped her hair back over her shoulder. "I thought you'd like it."

"It's not all that easy being on camera all the time," Logan told her.

"And it's not easy doing chores," she replied.

"At least you don't have people watching you all the time," he said.

"At least you don't have to shovel horse manure," she shot back.

"Really, Becca?" he asked. "Have you seen our show? Some of those lines . . ."

After half a second of shocked silence, she laughed. "You win. Come on." She held out her hand. "Let's go jump some more."

I shook my head. Figures. Another Logan groupie. Although I had to admit, he handled Becca's attitude much better than I did. I had to give him credit for that. But it didn't mean I wasn't just the slightest bit jealous.

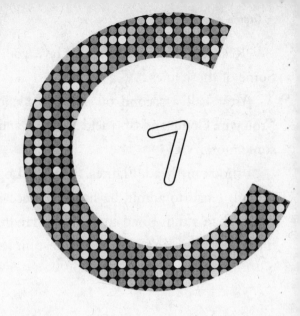

Mom and Dad had gotten back from

Mansfield while we were at the creek. They were sitting in the bunkhouse reading when I got back.

"Ah, there she is," Dad said.

Mom looked up from her book. "Did you have a good time? Looks like you got some sun."

"Yes and yes," I told her, and headed to my room.

"You'll want to take a quick shower and get dressed," she called after me. "Liz wants to meet in the dining hall before dinner to film the questions and answers for Ask Cass."

I stopped dead in my tracks. "For what?"

Dad lowered the paper he was reading. "The questions

for that website. Liz told you about it this morning," he said. "Don't you remember?"

"She said I'd be answering questions from readers. She didn't tell me they were calling it 'Ask Cass.' And she didn't say anything about taping it. I thought maybe I'd be writing them out or something."

Mom set aside her book. "If you're uncomfortable with it—"

"I'm fine," I assured her. "Just surprised, is all." Though I probably shouldn't have been. I did everything on camera. A free afternoon at the creek was not something I should get used to. Liz would have sent Ty along to spy on us if she had been around.

"She'd like you to wear one of the new outfits you'll find hanging in your closet," Mom said.

One of the outfits Becca had put away for me earlier, I realized. "Super," I muttered.

"What?"

"I will."

"Oh, look at you!" Liz crowed. "Very cute. And that blue will show up nicely on camera."

I smoothed the front of my shirt, glad she hadn't noticed I'd ditched the little scarf that had come with it. Toying with my charm necklace, I looked back to where Bayani and Ty had set up a mini studio in the rear of the dining hall, next to a large window. "So this is where we're doing it, huh?" I asked. Duh.

"Yes." She slipped an arm around my shoulders. "Come on back, and we'll get you wired and ready to go."

While Ty connected my lav mic, Bayani adjusted the angle of the big wingback chair I would be sitting in so that it got "the best light." Next to the chair stood a little tea table, and on the table sat a stack of white index cards.

"These are the questions sent in by their readers," Liz told me. "You'll want to read the question out loud, set down the card, look directly into the camera, and answer the question as if you're having a conversation with the audience."

"Except it's not really a conversation."

"Pardon?"

"I mean, no one's here but me," I said, "so it's going to be more like a monologue than a conversation."

Her smile went plastic, and she patted me on the back. "Whatever you'd like to call it," she said in a forced tone, "just be personable and talk to the camera. Understand?"

I shrugged. "Sure." I mean, how hard could it be?

Settling on the chair, I picked up the index cards and started to shuffle through them. Two cards in, I caught Logan's name and was just about to read the question when Bayani cleared his throat.

I glanced up, and he pointed to Ty, who was counting down with his fingers . . . three, two, one. Then he pointed to me as a signal I was on. I looked from his fingers to the red, blinking record light, to the lens of the camera.

And went completely blank.

Was I supposed to give some kind of greeting or introduction? Liz hadn't said anything about that. Should I just read the questions? I looked to her, and she gave me the move-it-along gesture. Not helpful. I'd have to wing it.

"Hi," I said into the camera. "I'm Cassidy. Thanks for sending in your questions." I held up the index cards in illustration. "Here we go."

Since the index card with Logan's name on it was now on top, I started with that one. "What's it like to work with Logan McCarthy?" Great. How was I supposed to answer that one? Fun? Frustrating? The most honest answer was probably a combination of the two. But then, whoever wrote the question probably wasn't interested in the most honest answer. She was probably like the groupies who swarmed him in Mansfield, which meant she wanted the inside scoop on Logan, but only the good stuff. "Logan's the greatest," I said. "We've been friends for years, so it's not really work hanging out with him."

There. Upbeat. Mostly honest. I moved on to the next card. "What's Logan's favorite color?" Well, at least that one I didn't have to think about. "Blue." Which is why I liked to wear blue a lot. But no one needed to know that.

Next card. "What kind of girl does Logan like?" I could actually feel the smile freeze on my face. Seriously. It made my lips go numb. Again, I thought of the girls in Mansfield. Logan's silly grin. "He likes all sorts of girls," I said, "especially those who are enthusiastic and who show an interest in him."

Gag.

On and on it went. Not that I was keeping score, but at least three-quarters of the questions I answered were about Logan. (All right, so maybe I did keep score: five questions about me or the show, sixteen about Logan.) By the time we were done, I should have charged him for being his publicist. It was insane.

"Very nicely done," Liz said. "This will be great exposure for the minisodes. And I'm sure as we go along, the number of questions will only increase."

"As we go along?"

"Oh, yes," she said brightly. "They'd like Ask Cass to be a recurring feature for their online content."

Another frozen smile. Super. That's all I needed—more sessions for me to answer questions about Logan. But it was for the good of the show, right? And the more successful the show was, the more time Logan and I would get to spend together. "That's great," I told Liz. "Looking forward to it."

"So, how'd it go?" Logan asked me after dinner.

I toyed with my dessert. "It was fine."

He laughed. "Fine? Way to play it down. Bayani said they want this to be a regular thing. You're a star."

I rolled my eyes. Right.

"So what did they ask you? What kinds of questions did you get?"

"What? Bayani didn't tell you that, too?" I asked.

Logan frowned. "Uh, no. That's why I'm asking you."

"Oh. Well . . ." How much should I tell him? I saw the way he reacted to the screaming groupies; I could just imagine what kind of big head he'd get if he knew about his online fandom as well. "Uh . . ."

The sound of a *ping, ping, ping!* from behind us saved me from having to give him an answer. I turned away from Logan to look up at Cavin, who stood at the head of his table, tapping the side of his glass with a spoon. He had asked us all to stay behind for a special meeting after the rest of the guests had cleared the mess hall.

"May I have everyone's attention, please," he said. "We have an announcement to make."

Once everyone quieted down, Cavin set down his spoon. He kept the glass in his hand though, and raised it toward Bayani, whose face had gone deep red. "We've just learned," he said dramatically, "that our own Bayani has been selected to receive the Bonner Award for Excellence for the Valencia episode. Despite lost luggage and equipment and Jack being out, Bayani pulled together an award-winning production. Just goes to show you how it's pressure what makes a diamond." He raised his glass higher. "To Bayani. Cheers!"

I picked up my water glass for the toast. Logan clinked it with his.

"I just love Spain," Deena said. "I was there a few years back, on the makeup team for *Quantum of Solace.* You know, that James Bond film with Daniel Craig? He is amazing. And those eyes!" She pressed her hand to her heart as if she was going to swoon.

"I saw that movie," Logan said. "Where was it filmed?"

"I worked on the crew in Madrid," Deena told him. "Is that near Valencia?"

Daniel harrumphed. "Not even close."

"Oh, pardon me." Deena brushed a pink strand of hair from her eyes so she could glare at him. "How foolish of me to ask."

"It's called geography," Daniel muttered.

I think he was going to say something else, but Ty interrupted him by yelling, "Speech! Speech!"

Bayani hesitated for a minute, but Cavin and my mom and dad practically pushed him out of his seat.

"Thanks, you guys," he said. "I couldn't have done it without the world's best crew, so this award really belongs to all of us."

He kept going, thanking everyone from the network's top executives to the support staff—even though none of them were around to hear it.

Deena giggled and made a comment about how Bayani sounded like he was giving an acceptance speech for an

Academy Award. Several of us within earshot laughed. Except Daniel.

"What would you know about the Academy Awards?" he hissed to Deena. "Don't tell me. You've done makeup for the presenters, right?"

"Daniel," Jack said in a low voice. "Calm down, man."

"If you'll excuse me," Daniel said. "I need some air." He got up and walked out the door. Could have been he wasn't feeling well, but it looked more like he was angry. And I didn't think it was because Deena mentioned the Academy Awards.

"I'll be right back," I said, and hurried after Daniel. I found him speed-walking behind the dining hall. "Hey, are you all right?"

"Me?" He kept walking. "I'm perfect. Fine. Just peachy."

"Daniel. Come on. It's me."

He stopped just short of the light that spilled out from the open kitchen door. "You really want to know? It's the way everyone flocks to that girl." He said the word sourly, and I knew he meant Deena. "Laughing at her jokes, standing up for her."

"Oh. I'm sorry," I said lamely.

"Yeah, well . . ."

"I'm sure no one meant to hurt your feelings."

He shook his head. "I'm not concerned about feelings. I'm concerned about someone else doing my job."

I watched him walk away, and I was pretty sure I knew

how he felt. I used to be the popular one with the network. Now Logan was their golden boy. No one asked me if I was ready to be replaced, either.

"Is he all right?" The kitchen doorway framed Riley as he undid the ties of his server's apron.

"He will be."

Riley hung the apron on a hook by the door and, after a quick glance over his shoulder, slipped out of the kitchen.

"You done for the night?" I asked him.

"If we hurry I am." He waved for me to follow him and jogged around the side of the building.

I forgot all about how I had told Logan and everyone I'd be back, and followed Riley. We slowed to a walk after we were out of sight of the dining hall.

"Got drama, huh?" Riley asked.

For a second I thought he could read my mind about Logan, but after a beat or two, it registered that he was talking about Daniel. "Oh, yeah. Some hurt feelings, I think."

"That sucks."

"It does," I agreed. "So where are we going?"

He glanced back at the dining hall. "Anywhere but there. Dad's cheesed about something tonight. I'm done being yelled at."

"Oh. I'm sorry." I didn't know what else to say. I thought to ask why his dad was "cheesed," but it wasn't any of my business. Nothing else I could think of sounded any better in my mind, so I just kept my mouth shut.

And so did he. We walked for a while without saying anything. Which was okay. Sometimes you don't need to fill the empty space with words.

Up ahead, a man sat on a bench in front of one of the bunkhouses, under the glow of the porch light. He was bent over a long piece of wood, and from the flash, flash, flash, of something metallic catching the light, I guessed he was carving something. Since he was looking down, his hat shaded his face, but I thought I recognized the hat.

"Is that Malo?" I asked.

"Yeah," Riley said. "Working on his stick again."

"His what?"

"He's got this walking stick. Picked it up in the bush a coupla years ago, and he's been carving and painting on it ever since. Come on. I'll ask him to show you."

Malo looked up as we got closer and nodded at us. Just the way Logan did whenever he saw me, I thought with a pang.

"Told Hollywood here about your stick," Riley told Malo. "Mind if we take a gander?"

"No worries." He held it out to us so that we could see. It was pretty big to be called a stick—maybe three or four inches around, and at least five feet tall. Relief carvings decorated the top third of it, and the rest was decorated with dots of paint. Both the carvings and dot paintings looked like the kind of thing you might see in a cave drawing, with animals and symbols and stuff. Only instead of woolly mammoths or bison, there were kangaroos and snakes and a tree with a really wide top.

"It's amazing," I told Malo. "What do all the symbols mean?"

"They are from the Dreamtime stories," he said. "These are the First People's stories of creation." He pointed out some symbols that represented thunder and lightning, snakes, kangaroos, and a whole bunch of other animals.

I ran my fingers over the painted end. Some parts had been worn smooth, but others must have been newer, because the paint still felt like small bumps on the wood. "I love how you made the pictures with dots," I said.

"It comes from the sand drawings they used to do, right Malo?" Riley asked.

He nodded. "Sacred stories were told by pictures drawn in the sand," he said. "Quickly erased so outside eyes couldn't see."

"And these pictures?" I asked.

"Only symbols of the Dreamtime. Not the sacred stories."

I turned the stick around and around to follow the flow of the dot figures and the carved creatures on top. "This is the coolest thing I've ever seen."

Malo chuckled. "Thank you."

"I mean it. It's amazing."

"Then you must have it," Malo said. He pushed it toward me, but I backed away.

"Oh, no. I didn't mean . . . I couldn't take it from you. Besides," I joked, "I don't think it would fit in my suitcase."

He thought for a moment, then leaned onto the stick and stood up. "Come with me."

We followed him into his bunkhouse. Only one bed, I noticed. Malo probably didn't have to share with the other station hands since he was the foreman. Along one whole wall stood a rough wooden workbench that held paint pots, more carved pieces, and what almost looked like a giant version of his walking stick, except that it was about four times as big around, and tapered narrower on one end. It was also hollow. Every inch of it was decorated with the dot paintings.

"That's Malo's didgeridoo." Riley told me.

"Oh, I've heard of those. It's a musical instrument, right?"

"I don't know how musical it is," Riley said.

"Off with ya." Malo swatted at Riley, and then he turned to me. "You're right, Miss Cassidy. It is for making music."

"Do you play it?" I asked. "Can I hear?"

He considered for a moment. "Perhaps just a bit." Taking the instrument from his workbench, Malo sat on a stool in the corner of the room and settled the didgeridoo in front of him, the wider end reaching the floor. He bobbed his head a few times, like he was counting the beat in his head, then pursed his lips, brought the didgeridoo to his mouth, and blew.

A low, deep note vibrated right through me, again, again, again. Malo played in short bursts, drumming the side of the long instrument with his fingers, feet tapping out the rhythm on the floor. I found myself moving to the beat, too. It wasn't even a song, really, but it made me want to dance.

But then, with one last reverberating note, the music stopped. Malo sat for a moment, letting it fade into nothing, and then he stood. "Right, so that's the didge."

"He made it," Riley said.

"Very cool," I told them both.

"But loud," Malo said, smiling. "Not much call for playing it around here. And not what I intended to show you."

After carefully laying the instrument back on his workbench, Malo pulled out a plastic box and opened the lid. "I think I have something you might like."

The box rattled a bit as he dug through it, then he held out his palm to show me a small wooden circle about the size of a nickel. A double circle had been painted on the wood, surrounded by several smaller circles so that it looked like a flower or a sunburst. "This," Malo said, pointing to the larger center circle, "represents where the Dreaming comes from."

"Ooh," I breathed. "Look at that detail."

"It's yours," Malo said. When I hesitated, he laughed, his dark eyes crinkling around the edges. "Surely this will fit in your suitcase."

I took the little wooden disk from him. The wood was warm and smooth in my hand. "Yes, it will. Thank you!"

Malo gestured with his chin. "If you want, I could fashion a loop for it, so you can put it on that necklace of yours."

"Yes, please. That would be perfect." I handed the disk back to him, and he set it on the bench. He rustled through the box again and pulled out a spool of wire, cutting off a short length that he made into a teeny loop. He poked a hole into the wood with what looked like a large needle, and forced the twisted end of the wire into the opening.

He waved me off when I tried to thank him again. "You just remember the Dreaming, and it will always be with you."

I wasn't sure exactly what that meant, but I promised him I would remember, and we said good night. As Riley and I left Malo's bunkhouse, I unhooked the clasp on my necklace so I could tie the charm onto the leather cord.

"Sure got a lot of them on there," Riley said, looking over my shoulder.

"Yeah," I said. "I pick one up from every place we travel."

"Pretty soon there'll be too many to fit around your neck," he joked, "then you'll have to start another one."

I curled my fingers around the charms protectively. "I could never replace this one; my grampa made it for me. He even gave me the first charm." I found the silver Italian horn at the center of the collection and showed it to Riley.

He dutifully admired the charm, even if he wasn't quite as interested in the history of the necklace as I was. I reached back to hook the cord back around my neck, but I couldn't get the clasp to close properly.

"Can you look at this?" I asked Riley. I turned my back to him and lifted my hair so he could fasten the clasp for me.

That's when I saw Logan.

"Hey, there you are," Logan said. "We wondered what happened to you." His words were meant for me, but he was clearly looking at Riley.

"Went for a walk," I said. "Malo showed us the didgeridoo he made."

"Is that what I heard?" Logan looked beyond Riley to the bunkhouse. "I was just coming to see what it was."

"Yeah." I told Logan about how Malo had made the didge, and explained about the Dreamtime dot paintings, but I could tell Logan wasn't listening. His eyes kept straying to Riley. Like he was sizing him up. Like he was jealous.

That last idea made me smile. Good. Let Logan feel what it's like for a while.

• • • • •

So what did you do? Zoe asked when we texted that night.

I said good night and came back to my room, I typed.

Her answer was immediate. **You leave him standing alone???**

I smiled as I send the reply. **Not alone. Riley was there. :)**

But . . . why? she texted.

It's good for him, I wrote back. **He should get to know Riley better. Besides, a little jealousy never hurt anyone.**

The next morning found me sitting on the tree stump in the yard by myself, watching the sun come up. I'd been so into the idea of Logan being jealous, I forgot to ask him if he was going to join me. Which served me right, I supposed. It wasn't very nice of me to leave him standing there with Riley. Not nice to him, and not nice to Riley.

I planned to apologize to both of them at breakfast, but Logan never showed up—Cavin said he had slept in—and I only caught glimpses of Riley rushing around in the kitchen. Then it was time for lessons, and Victoria pulled me away, so I never got a chance to see him after that.

I kept waiting for a chance to talk to Logan during class, but Victoria never gave us a break. We were supposed to go riding at noon, and she wanted to fit everything in before Liz came to tell us to get ready.

So that's how I ended up in front of the makeup mirror, sneaking peeks at where Logan sat playing a game on his phone while Deena did her thing with my face. She was telling me about some movie set she worked on, but the words all mushed together. All I could think about was Logan.

Finally, Deena took my chin and turned my face to hers. "Hello? Cassidy, I'm talking to you."

"Oh. I'm sorry. I was just . . ."

"I think I can guess." She leaned in closer and whispered. "I've seen the way you've been looking at him all morning. He is a cutie."

My face must have gone pinker than her hair. "That's not what I . . . He's just a . . ."

"It's okay," Deena said, patting my hand. "Your secret's safe with me. Now pucker up."

"I'm sorry?"

"The lip butter." She held up a tiny pot and a lip brush. "You like it? It's called 'kissable pink.'"

I must have looked horrified because she laughed and patted me on the hand again. "Oh, come on. I'm just teasing. Although if you ever do want me to make your lips look kissable—"

"Deena!" I slid a quick look at Logan, hoping he hadn't heard. His head remained bent over his game.

Still chuckling, she brushed back my hair. "Yep. You've got it bad." I flinched, and she leaned close again. "Don't worry," she said quietly. "I promised I wouldn't tell. Girlfriends have to stick together."

Girlfriends? I looked back at her, and she gave me a

cheesy smile. And when I didn't immediately smile back, she crossed her eyes and stuck her tongue out to the side. I couldn't help laughing then.

"There we go," she said. "Feels better, doesn't it?" She hummed to herself as she brushed my hair, watching my face through the mirror. I tried not to disappoint her by letting the smile slip, even when Logan stood up from his chair and walked over to talk to Riley. She must have felt me tense up or something, though, because her fingers sped up as she finished the braid. "All done!" she proclaimed. "Almost." She handed me an Aussie-style cowboy hat. "Liz brought this by for you. She wants you to wear this on the trail today,"

I set the hat on my head and adjusted the angle, frowning at my reflection in the mirror. Don't get me wrong: the hat was awesome. It had the same low brim and rolled sides as the one I had liked so much on Becca. But that was just it: that hat was on Becca. It *fit* Becca. She was a real jillaroo, not me. I just looked like I was pretending.

"She left you this as well," Deena said, handing me a folded piece of paper.

I opened it up to find a short note in Liz's slanted handwriting. The hat was a gift from a local manufacturer. Not exactly a sponsor, but they advertised on the stations that would carry *When in Rome*.

Which meant I would wear the hat, no matter how ridiculous I felt in it.

In fact, I felt ridiculous in the entire outfit. From the

square-toed boots to the jeans to the tank top I wore under the short-sleeve plaid shirt—everything I had on was a gift from one sponsor or another. The only thing that was mine was my charm necklace. I settled that on top of the tank top so at least I could remember who I was.

I lost track of Logan and Riley while Ty was wiring my lav mic. They were standing together by a eucalyptus tree one minute, and then Ty turned me around so he could tape my transmitter to my side. When I looked again, they were gone.

Mom and Dad strolled by just as Ty finished wiring my lav mic.

"Oh, I like the hat," Mom said. "It will keep the sun off your face."

"The costume is very cute," Dad added.

"Great," I muttered, and pushed out of the chair.

"Did I say something wrong?" Dad asked Mom. "Cute's not a bad thing, is it?"

Mom patted his arm. "It's fine, dear."

I saw Logan and Riley by the big eucalyptus tree and escaped Mom and Dad to go join them. Logan was wearing his going-riding outfit, too, but on him it looked . . . really good, actually. And definitely not as out of place as I felt.

He tipped his hat to me when he saw me coming. "So what do you think?"

"It's a good look for you," I told him sincerely.

"You, too," he said. "I like the boots."

I flushed and dug the toe of one of those boots in the dust. "Thanks." Funny how I could go from completely angsty to totally happy just because Logan said I looked good.

But then Riley had to go and spoil it by laughing. "What, you never seen hats or boots before?"

"What about hats and boots?" Becca asked as she strolled up beside us.

"Nothing," I said quickly. I hoped the guys would take my cue and drop the subject. One word from Becca and I'd be right back to feeling stupid in my jillaroo getup.

Thankfully, she wasn't interested enough to pursue it. "Right, then," she said. "Come on. Let's get over to the stables. It's about time to ride out."

"You *have* seen a horse before, right?" Riley teased.

"What are you talking about?" Becca asked.

"It's nothing," I told her again, and shot Riley a look. "Tell us about the ride. Where will we be going?"

"Off the flats and into the hills," Riley answered. "Show you a bit of wild Australia."

"Will we see kangaroos?" I asked hopefully. I had seen some a long time ago in the zoo back in Ohio, but that didn't count because they had been in an enclosure so I never got to see one really jump.

Becca rolled her eyes. "You're such a tourist! What do you think? We run a petting farm?" She looked to Riley and scoffed. "Few palings short of a fence, this one."

A furnace lit up in my face. "Oh. I just thought—"

"Yeah, I know what you thought. You Yanks are all alike. One step off the plane, and you expect to find boomers hopping all over the place. They do have habitats, you know."

Well, of course they did. I knew that. But I kind of figured their habitat was . . . Australia. I mean, you think of Australia, and you think of kangaroos, right? But it's a big continent. It made sense they wouldn't be everywhere.

She huffed self-righteously and turned to Logan. "Next she'll be asking me to pet the koalas."

And he laughed. He *laughed*, the jerk.

"Excuse me." I folded my arms and glared at him. "I seem to remember someone searching the trees for koalas yesterday."

"Aw, come on," he said, completely sidestepping my comment. "Don't take everything so personally."

I can't even tell you how much I wanted to snap at him at that moment. But not more than five feet away stood Ty holding that stupid camera, a too-clear reminder that everything we did and said was being recorded. I bit back the words and smiled sweetly at Logan instead. "Thanks for the advice."

Travel tip: In Australia, it's all about a fair go, the great outdoors, and a healthy helping of irony.

I should have known I was in for trouble the moment the ranch hands led our horses from the stables. Especially when one of them brought out a big, burly black horse that looked like he was in a bad mood.

Becca directed the station hand to bring the horse to me. "This is Bunyip," she told me, "I think you'll like him."

He looked worried. (The station hand, not the horse.) "You an experienced rider?" he asked.

I slipped a quick peek at Becca, who was watching a little too eagerly. Waiting for me to fail, I realized. "Yes," I told the station hand. "I grew up riding horses." Which wasn't a complete lie. I mean, my gramma and grampa had horses on their farm when I was younger, and I used to ride them. Not all the time, but Grampa had given me some training, so I knew what I was doing. I even went riding in Costa Rica not long ago. Of course, my trusty steed then was the granddaddy horse on the farm, but Becca didn't have to know that. I smiled at her with more confidence than I felt and climbed onto the saddle.

The horse tossed his head and snorted angrily as I settled onto his back, and the guy's hand tightened around the reins. "Dunno, miss. I could get you another mount," he offered.

"I'm good," I told him, which was kind of hard to do with my heart lodged in my throat.

Logan patted his perfectly docile horse on the neck and gave me a worried look. "I could trade with you, if you want."

Aw. So sweet. So protective. And so not anything I was going to accept in front of Becca. "Seriously. I'm going to get along just fine with . . . what was his name again?"

"Bunyip," Riley said.

"Bunyip," I repeated. I tried to pat him on the neck the way Logan had done to his horse, but Bunyip turned his head and snapped at me. I yanked my hand away.

"Bunyip was named after a monster that lives in the outback," Becca said. "He lives up to his name." She turned her horse to trot out of the enclosure and called over her shoulder, "Enjoy the ride!"

Once everyone had a horse and got the hang of the saddle, we met in front of the stables so we could ride out together. A camera had been mounted on the back of one of the ATVs Logan, Riley, Becca, and I had ridden the day before. Daniel was elected to be the designated driver, while Ty manned the camera.

The whole thing must have been something to see, because several people from the other groups staying at the ranch had gathered around to watch (and snap pictures). Camera Guy, of course, was front and center. I clung to Bunyip's reins with a white-knuckled grip and tried to keep him turned so that we were facing away from the curious onlookers and their cameras. The last thing I needed was my terrified expression all over the Internet. Bunyip, of course, didn't cooperate, so I was sure there would soon be plenty of unflattering images to find their way onto tumblr and instagram.

None of it seemed to bother Liz. She continued to give direction from the back of her (very calm) horse. "Your mics have been masked to block the noise from the ATV engines," she told Logan and me, "but we'll still be able to pick up your voices, so I'd like to see you try to talk to each other as often as you can. Describe the experience. That sort of thing."

Ha. One look at the way Bunyip flattened his ears and whipped his tail, and I could guess what kind of experience he (and Becca) had in mind for me.

"I'm serious, Cass," Logan said in a low voice. "If you want to trade—"

Mr. Calder saved me from having to make the decision. "What do ya know?" he said loudly, to get everyone's attention. "We've got Christmas on a stick for ya this morning!"

"He means, we've got something special," Riley explained to me. "Kind of a treat."

"A pack of brumbies were spotted this morning out on the ridge," Mr. Calder said. "We're going to bring 'em in. Now, if you'd like, we can turn our ride today into a roundup. Who's game?"

Deena spoke for all of us with a loud "Yeehaw!" At least she spoke for most of us. The way Bunyip kept shifting beneath me, I wasn't so sure. But what was I going to say with the cameras and the people (and Becca) watching for my reaction?

"You should know," Mrs. Calder cautioned, "that the

brumbies are fast and wily. We'll be chasing them at a full gallop, so if any of you are uncomfortable with that, you can hold back and watch, no questions asked."

During Mrs. Calder's entire speech, Bunyip kept stomping and snorting and tossing his head, and I swear he knew exactly what she was saying, because the moment she said the word *chasing,* his muscles tensed up and he clopped anxiously like he was ready to bolt. When I tried to get him to settle down by pulling back on the reins, he sidestepped and pinned my leg up against the fence. It didn't hurt, but it made me look like an idiot, not being able to control my horse.

"If at *any* time you are uncomfortable," Mr. Calder repeated (looking straight at me, I might add), "give us the signal, like this." He raised one hand into the air. "We'll help you rein in your mount."

Becca turned to me, all wide eyes and fake concern. "You're sure you'll be okay?"

I tightened my knees against Bunyip's sides and even though I couldn't get him to budge away from the fence, I lifted my chin and pretended I was in control. "No worries," I told her.

I just hoped I was right.

Starting out wasn't too bad. Bunyip clearly didn't like me on his back, but at least he didn't try to throw me off or anything. He wouldn't do a thing I wanted him to do, but that wasn't such a big deal since we were riding in one long line, and all he had to do was follow the other horses. That he could do by himself.

It was pretty easy going at that point, anyway. The land around the bunkhouses and outbuildings was mostly flat and open, with the exception of a few clusters of eucalyptus trees and some low scrub bushes. The horses walked at an easy gait, so all we had to do was not fall off the saddle. Easy. I allowed myself to relax a little.

I had to admit that it was an absolutely perfect day to be riding. The sky stretched overhead, perfect and clear and

Easter-egg blue. The sun was warm, but not hot (yet). A breath of a breeze ruffled Bunyip's mane and whispered through the tiny holes in my hat. Hard to believe it was January. Back at Gramma's farm in Ohio, there was probably about a foot of snow on the ground, and the sky would be steel-gray until spring.

I must have relaxed a little too much, because Ty called out from the camera ATV as it pulled alongside Bunyip and me, "Cass! Look alive!"

Bunyip either didn't like the noise or the dust or the closeness of the strange men on the wheeled thing or something, because he snorted, reared back, and shook his head so hard that the reins whipped out of my hands. I yelped and reached for them, but I wasn't quick enough. I had to grab handfuls of Bunyip's mane so I wouldn't fall off.

Riley was beside me in an instant. "Ey! Ey! Ey! Ey!" He crowded close to us and grabbed Bunyip's bridle until my monster horse settled down.

Ty and Daniel were smart enough to zip ahead of us or they would have gotten a death glare from me. They still might get the glare later, depending on how much of the event Ty had captured on camera.

It was about that time that we passed the first fence line. A couple of the station hands were out repairing a fence pole, and they stopped to watch us as we rode by. One of them met my eye and grinned as he tipped his hat. It was an innocent enough gesture, but I couldn't help but feel like he was laughing at me. And how could he not, after seeing how I nearly lost control of my horse? The entire group of us probably looked pretty silly—obvious city folk on our way out to a roundup, trying to play jackaroo.

Well, I figured, if everything about me already screamed tourist, I may as well embrace the role. I quickly dug my phone out of my pocket and snapped a picture of the laughing hat-tipper. This would have been a great addition to my blog if Bunyip hadn't double-stepped beneath me again just as the shutter whirred open and closed. Then he threw his head back and snorted, as if he knew he had ruined my shot and was proud of it. Great. Now my horse was laughing at me, too.

I would have tried for another shot, but Bunyip, who had apparently decided he'd had enough of our slow-moving line, chose that moment to start trotting, and I needed both my hands to hang on. I stuffed my phone back into my pocket—no easy task while bouncing up and down in the saddle—and double-fisted the reins.

"Hey!" Becca called as we passed her. "You're supposed to stay in line!"

I looked back at her and shrugged. Let her think I was breaking the rules or whatever. It was better than my admitting I had no control. Seriously. Bunyip had a mind of his own—which was exactly why Becca had chosen him for me. It didn't matter if I pulled back on his reins or tried to steer him right or left. He just kept barreling ahead, picking up speed, as if he already knew where we were going.

"Slow down!" my dad yelled.

"No worries," Mr. Calder shouted. "He must smell the brumbies. Come on!" He spurred his own horse into a gallop, and all the other horses followed automatically.

The farther we got from the main houses, the hillier the land became. Soon, we were galloping up hills and down gullies, and after I got the hang of it, I have to admit it was kind of fun. Especially when the ground got too bumpy for the ATV to handle without damaging the camera equipment, and they had to veer off. Ty would just have to film from a distance.

Riley rode alongside me again. I wondered if he thought I'd lost control once more, so I was about to signal him that I was doing fine, thank you, when he pointed ahead. "There they are!"

My breath caught right in my throat. On the ridge stood about two dozen of the most beautiful, proud, rugged-looking horses I had ever seen. They ranged in color from dusty brown to chestnut to dappled gray, and they were all sleek and well muscled. They held their heads high, watching us, nostrils flared. And then, as if they'd been given a signal, they took off all at once down the other side of the ridge, away from us.

I don't know about anyone else, but I didn't have to coax Bunyip into running after the brumbies. In fact, I didn't have to give him any kind of a hint at all. He obviously already knew the game. I held on for dear life as he raced down the hill.

Riley pulled ahead of me, and I watched him for a moment, noticing how he had shifted position in the saddle to move with his horse as they started the chase. I tried to mimic him, shifting my weight forward, pushing up on the stirrups, gripping the reins close to the back of Bunyip's neck. Then I let Bunyip take over instead of fighting him for control, and I found the rhythm in his stride. Soon, we were flying over the hills like a team, closing in on the brumbies. I had no idea what we'd do once we reached them, but I'm pretty sure Bunyip did. I figured I might as well let him do his thing and just enjoy the ride.

It was so well orchestrated, I swear the roundup could have been a scene in a movie. Mr. Calder, Malo, Ryan, and Riley hemmed the horses in on both sides, which forced them to run down a gully. The gully turned into a dead end. Once the horses were trapped, Mr. Calder and Malo rode around and around them, cracking long whips until the herd huddled together.

"What will you do with them now?" I asked Riley. I guessed they couldn't be brought into the stables with the other horses until they were tamed.

"They'll go to the north pasture," Riley said, "until we have a chance to work with them."

"Do you do this a lot?"

"What? Round them up? I guess. Whenever there's a mob to be found . . ."

"Where do you put them all?" I asked.

He looked at me blankly for a second. "The north pasture," he repeated.

"And then what?"

He pushed his hat back and squinted at me. "I don't follow."

"You know," I coaxed, "if you keep gathering up brumbies and putting them in the north pasture, pretty soon they're going to take over, right? So I was just wondering what you did with them. Like, do you tame them and find them new homes, do you relocate them off the property, or what?"

"Oh. Right." He studied the horses for a moment. "Have you heard about the brumby debate in these parts?"

I shook my head. "There's a debate?"

"Yeah. See, horses aren't native to Australia. The British brought 'em over with the first fleet. Brumbies come from that stock—escaped or were let go or something—and they went wild. Now, a coupla hundred years later, there's too many. Some people call them feral pests. They say the brumbies harm the environment, so they want to control the population."

The way he said control made my insides shrink. "How?"

He looked away. "Hunting. Trapping . . ."

"They *kill* them?" I whispered. I almost felt like covering Bunyip's ears when I said it.

Riley swallowed hard. "Hundreds and hundreds of them. My mom and dad think there's another way: domesticate and relocate."

"Oh." I sat a little straighter in the saddle. So in a way, we hadn't just helped to round up wild horses; we had helped to save them.

Logan rode up beside us. "Man, wasn't that awesome?" His face was flushed, and his hat had blown back and was hanging around his neck by the chin strap.

"Glad you think so," Riley said. "'cause we're not done. We still have to get them to the paddock."

"Do I get to crack a whip?" Logan asked.

His smile and his enthusiasm were contagious. Riley's serious expression gave way to a grin. "Sure. Come on, I'll show you how."

I didn't even notice that Becca was there until I turned my horse to follow Logan and Riley.

"Oh, hey," I told her. "Thanks for choosing Bunyip for me. He was the perfect horse for a ride like this."

Travel tip: If you are teased, Australians expect you to take it with good humor. Such self-confidence will increase their respect for you.

The ride to the north pasture wasn't as exciting as the

chase, obviously, but it was fun watching Logan try to swing Riley's long stock whip to make it crack. Riley explained that the whips weren't actually used to hit the horses they were herding (or mustering, as Riley called it). They used the whips to make a loud *crack!*, and the horses would move to get away from the sound.

Actually making that cracking sound took some skill, though. I found that out the hard way when Logan caught me giggling at one of his attempts.

He wound the whip up and held it out to me. "I'd like to see you try," he challenged.

I took the whip awkwardly. The stock was solid in my hand, but the whip part must have been at least eight feet long. I could just see myself getting tangled up in it or whipping myself. Or whipping Bunyip, which would probably be worse because then he would bolt. "Um, how . . . ?"

"Swing it back over your shoulder," Riley said, "then forward as fast as you can."

I did as he said, but the whip just kind of flopped back and forth because it was too long to get much speed out of it. Same result when I tried again.

Becca rode up alongside me. "Here," she demanded, holding out her hand. "Let me show you how it's done."

What else could I do? I handed over the whip.

She galloped off maybe five yards or so and then wheeled her horse around so she was facing us. When she swung the whip back, it sailed overhead in a graceful arc, swirling in a half circle like a lasso before snapping back downward. The *crack!* was loud and crisp.

Becca demonstrated a couple more times, each swing like a dance the way the whip curved up and back, so smooth, so elegant. She made it look easy, which I knew it wasn't.

"Wow," Logan said. Just one little word, but you should have heard how he said it. I shrank a little in my saddle.

I shrank even more when Daniel and Ty pulled up (but not too close) on the ATV.

"That was fantastic!" Ty said. He patted the camera. "I got the whole thing!"

Logan ignored them. "You've got to teach us how to do that," he said to Riley.

"When we're at camp," Riley said. "I can't teach you to whip while you're on a horse. You might hurt somebody."

"Wait," I said. "You just gave us the whip a minute ago. What was that?"

Riley gave me a sheepish smile. "Figured you couldn't do much damage if you can't even swing it proper."

Daniel threw his head back and laughed.

"Better watch it," Logan warned him. "You keep that up and you're liable to find out just how much damage she can do."

C 10

By the time we reached the north
pasture, Ty must have figured I'd had my quota of humili-
ation for the day because he put away the camera while
Daniel went to park the ATV. Riley and Becca rode off to
help herd the brumbies into the paddock, leaving Logan
and me alone for the first time all day.

And wouldn't you know, I couldn't think of anything to
say.

Stupid, right? I mean, there were a million things to
talk about. We'd just been on an amazing ride. We'd saved a
mob of brumbies. We had tried (and failed) to crack a whip.
And, of course, I still owed him that apology. I could have
said anything. But instead, I just sat there.

"Tired?" he asked me.

"The ride takes a lot out of you," I answered.

"Yeah. You'd think it wouldn't be so hard when the horses are the ones doing all the work."

"Yeah." Very eloquent.

I tried to come up with something better, but before I could redeem myself, one of the station hands came to take our horses and walk them over to their enclosure.

"You need help getting down?" he asked me.

I noticed he didn't ask Logan the same thing. "I'm fine," I insisted . . . and then just about fell out of the saddle as I tried to swing my leg over to dismount. I never imagined how stiff and sore I could get from being on horseback all day. It didn't even register while we were riding, but now that I was trying to move . . . The guy caught me before I hit the ground, but my pride did a face plant.

"Thanks," I told him.

He grinned at me the way that station hand by the fence had done earlier—obviously very amused by the klutzy tourist. "No worries," he said.

The guy led the horses away, leaving Logan and me alone again.

"Come on," Logan said, "let's walk it off."

We strolled (very stiffly) down to where the Calders had set up camp for the Aussie barbecue we'd be having that night. I was surprised to see Liz, Cavin, and Victoria already sitting on one of the log benches with Ty and Daniel, sipping cold drinks and chatting as if they were at a country club tea.

"When did you get here?" Logan asked his dad. "We were riding at the front of the muster, and I didn't see you at all."

"Ach, I'm too old to be chasin' after wild horses. I took it at an amble and watched the action from afar until Missus Calder brought us back here."

"Well, *I'm* not too old," Liz was quick to clarify. "Victoria and I rode as far as the gully."

"I haven't ridden that long or that hard for ages," Victoria agreed.

"After the horses were gathered together," Liz continued, "we figured you had it all under control. Ty was just telling us about the footage he got. I look forward to reviewing it."

Super. I could just imagine the episode they could put together with the kind of footage Ty got of me being smashed against the paddock fence, me losing control of Bunyip, me not being able to properly swing a whip . . .

But Logan wasn't worried about any of that. He turned to his dad. "You gotta see it, Da. It was awesome!"

I watched Logan talking about the ride and wished I could be more like him and not so self-conscious. He wouldn't worry about looking like an idiot on film as long as it was "real." Heck, he'd probably laugh about it. Why couldn't I do that?

"Cassidy?" Victoria nudged me. "I think you're being summoned." She pointed to where Mrs. Calder stood with my mom and dad by the grill. Bayani was mounting a camera to a rolling dolly nearby, and next to him Deena stood by the makeup chair, motioning for me to come over.

Apparently, it was time for a touch-up. So why wasn't she calling for Logan, too? If I needed one, then he— No. If I wanted to be more carefree like Logan, I couldn't worry about stuff like that.

I straightened and took a deep breath. "All right, I'm going in," I told Logan. "If I'm not out in ten, send backup."

He laughed and gave me a thumbs-up, and that was enough to make me happy. For a while.

Travel tip: Australia has one of the most diverse cuisines in the world, thanks to Asian and European migrant influences.

Mom did a segment with Mr. and Mrs. Calder, cooking our dinner on the barbecue grill (or the "ba-bee," as Mr. Calder called it). Which would have been fine if they hadn't kept starting and stopping, repeating lines (Mr. Calder kept wanting a redo whenever they wanted him to say, "throw another shrimp on the barbie." They weren't grilling shrimp, he insisted; they were grilling prawns. But Cavin was convinced that it would play better if they simply called the prawns shrimp.) And on and on. It was killing the rest of us. We could smell the food. We could see it piling up on the serving platters. But we couldn't eat it.

"We'll be done in a minute," Bayani kept saying. "It would interrupt the flow to stop and serve now."

But one minute turned into ten, and ten into twenty. And none of us were convinced there was any "flow" going on to be interrupted.

"Patience is a virtue," Victoria reminded us when Logan and I grumbled to each other. "Think of how good it will taste after all this anticipation."

"We've anticipated enough," Logan said. "I'm pretty sure it will taste good *now*."

Finally, Bayani and Cavin were satisfied and called the final "Cut!" Or maybe they had to wrap up because by then the sun was beginning to sink behind the hills and they were quickly losing light. Either way, they called it quits, and we were finally informed it was time to eat.

You've never seen such a mob scene as when we got the go ahead, and everyone grabbed their plates to line up for the food. The other thing about riding all day—besides making your butt really sore—is that it works up a mean appetite.

The good thing is that my mom and Mr. Calder had made a *lot* of food. For the segment they had just filmed, they wanted a good cross-section of "traditional" Australian cuisine. And since the population in Australia came from all over the world, that was a lot to cover.

We had everything from regular steaks to skewered Japanese *yaki niku* to Mediterranean-spiced chicken and lamb, plus a huge variety of grilled vegetables.

Victoria was right about the food tasting amazing after we'd had to wait so long to eat. By the time I filled my plate, I was completely drooling. I don't think I've ever been so focused on my dinner before in my life. I don't remember how I managed to get to the log bench where I sat to eat. I don't remember people around me talking. I must have been in a food stupor, because I managed to tune out all conversation until I had just about cleaned my plate.

And then I wished that I could tune it out again, because the first word that registered in my head was the word *flush*.

"The water's really supposed to swirl the other way when you flush?" Bayani was asking Logan.

"Yeah, but I watched," Logan said. "It didn't work."

I dropped my fork. "Really? This is what you guys about while you're eating? *Toilets?*"

"Well, yeah," Logan said, as if this was perfectly normal—and acceptable—dinner conversation. "They say that since we're on the other side of the equator, the water swirls the opposite direction than it does on our side. Something about the gravitational pull or something."

"The Coriolis effect," Victoria offered.

"Yeah. That."

"Sorry to disappoint you," she said, "but I'm afraid the Coriolis pull isn't great enough to affect the—"

"You, too, Victoria?" I tried to shake the entire subject out of my head.

"It wouldn't hurt you to take interest in scientific principles the way Logan is doing," she told me.

Right. Like Logan was interested in scientific principles.

Riley chuckled. "Besides, we don't have swirling dunnies at the ranch, mate."

"What?" Logan asked.

"Ours don't swirl." Riley talked slowly, like he was explaining to a three-year-old. "The water pushes straight down and out."

I stood up. "Okay. I am seriously done with this conversation."

"Wait." Riley grabbed my hand. "We'll change the subject."

I had no doubt that Riley would keep his word, but it was clear from the way Logan leaned forward, challenging, already drawing a breath to make his next point, that he wouldn't let it go so easily.

But whatever he was going to say dissolved, and his mouth clamped shut. Well, that was a nice change, I thought. Usually, Logan would keep it up just to bug me. Maybe he finally learned the art of backing down.

Or not.

Suddenly, I realized why Logan had stopped talking, and it had nothing to do with the topic of our conversation. He was staring at Riley's hand, where it still gripped mine.

Logan's eyebrow twitched, but otherwise his face went completely blank.

I flushed with pleasure at the thought that he could be jealous. That meant he cared, right? But then how come he wouldn't look at me after that? I kept trying to get his attention, but it's like he didn't even know I was there. Well, I wasn't going to just sit there being ignored. I looked around for somewhere else to go.

Near the fire pit, Mr. Calder was helping the station hands clean off the barbecue grill. Mrs. Calder was entertaining my mom and dad, Cavin, and Liz. Whatever she said had them laughing and wiping away tears. Closer to us, Ty, Deena, and Jack were bent over the camera in Jack's hand. It looked like they were comparing notes about something. They were all busy.

But being unnoticed by any of them would be better than being unnoticed by Logan. It would hurt less, anyway. He didn't even look up when I stood and walked away from the campfire. But Riley did. And he followed me.

"Where you going?" he asked.

I shrugged. "No place in particular. Just wanted to walk."

"Okay," he said, and fell into step beside me. He didn't try to talk, just walked along beside me for a while. As we neared the corral, he nudged me.

"There's Malo," he said. He pointed to the far corner of the corral. I could just see the foreman's outline perched on the fence railing, silhouetted in the moonlight.

"What's he doing?" I asked.

"Watching over the brumbies, I reckon," Riley said. "Come on."

We picked our way over the scrub in the darkness until we came to the fence line. Riley climbed up to sit on the rail, and I did the same—although my climbing was much shakier. And noisier. A few of the closest horses lifted their heads and looked at me with distrust.

"You're sure it's okay for us to sit facing the inside like this?" I whispered to Riley. "The brumbies won't charge us or anything?"

He chuckled softly. "Naw. They're really gentle. They wouldn't hurt—"

"Gentle? I thought they were wild."

He froze for a second, then caught himself. "Well, yeah. Of course. But . . . uh . . . Malo whispers to 'em. Keeps 'em calm. It's a native thing."

I eyed Malo dubiously. "I don't see him whispering any-thing."

"Well, sometimes all he has to do is watch over them and—"

"He's not even looking at them. He's whittling some-thing." Now that we were closer, I could see the knife blade flash as it caught the moonlight.

Riley chewed the corner of his lip. He wiped the palm of his hands on the front of his jeans. "Okay, look." He glanced over each shoulder and then leaned closer, even though there wasn't anyone else around—except Malo, and he was way on the far end of the corral. "You have to swear not to tell anyone."

"Tell anyone what?"

"Swear."

I drew a huge X across my chest. "Cross my heart. What is it?"

He hesitated a moment more and then said in a low voice, "These horses? They aren't really wild."

11

I stared at Riley. "You mean, these aren't brumbies?"

"Some of 'em were," he said quickly. "Or their sires were. But they've all been tame for some time now."

I laughed. Quietly, of course. "So the whole brumby run today?"

"Completely set up," Riley admitted. He glanced around again and then continued, "We gotta move the horses every few weeks to rotate the grazing, so . . ."

"So you might as well let the guests help," I finished for him.

"For the experience." He smiled sheepishly. "Mustering a bunch of horses from one end of the property to the other isn't that exciting, but rounding up brumbies? That gives 'em something to tell their friends back home."

"All part of the show," I agreed. "But what about all that other stuff you said? What about domesticate and relocate?"

"That's true. We really do bring in the wild ones and try to find new homes for them. But it's not something we could do with the tourist groups. Too dangerous."

"How is it different than what we did today?" I asked.

It was his turn to laugh. "That was a lark. The horses we rounded up are trained. They know the routine. Wild horses are unpredictable. Some of them will face you down like they've got something to prove."

Well, that was a little bit of a disappointment—I liked thinking I'd had a hand in saving wild horses—but it didn't take away from the thrill of the ride.

"You won't tell?" Riley asked.

"I promised, didn't I?"

He stared out at the dark shapes of the horses in the corral and nodded, like he was telling them it was going to be okay. "Thanks."

"No big," I told him. "Believe me, I get it. We do the same thing in my family."

He looked at me strangely, and I hurried to explain. "Even when I was a little kid, I was part of the family act," I told him. "Always had to be 'on.' Be the perfect TV family. It's all about giving people what they want."

"That's for dinky-di," he agreed.

"Don't get me wrong," I said. "I like doing the shows,

but sometimes I hate being so fake all the time, you know?"

He blew out his breath. "Tell me about it. Every summer, it's the same thing, the entire holiday: putting on for the tourists. Uh . . . Not that you . . . I mean . . ."

I waved his concern aside. "At least you only have to be part of the charade in the summer. I get to do it all year round."

"But you get to go places. See new things. For me, it's the same thing year after year."

I couldn't even imagine that. I'd been traveling with my mom and dad since I was young. But I could relate to sometimes feeling trapped.

"There you are!"

I jumped at the sound of Daniel's voice and nearly fell off the fence rail. "Don't ever do that!"

He just laughed. "Come on, Princess Cassidy. We need you on our team. You, too, bucko," he said to Riley.

I climbed down. Carefully. "Bucko? Really?"

"Hurry," he said, completely ignoring me. "We're about to start."

"Start what?" Riley asked.

"Charades. We need your acting skills."

Riley and I exchanged a look and burst out laughing.

"Don't worry," I told Daniel. "We've got you covered."

The tricky thing about charades with an international group is that not everyone has the same frame of reference.

I mean, Victoria grew up in London, Bayani in the Philippines, Logan and his dad are from Ireland, and the Calders live in the highlands of Australia. The rest of us are from the States, but even then, we don't all watch the same TV shows, read the same books, or see the same movies (unless we all happen to be on the same flight and awake during the in-flight entertainment). It quickly became obvious that we had to stick to classic books and movies if we had any hope of guessing what our teammates were talking about. The problem was, whose definition of classic were we supposed to use?

"It doesn't matter," Mrs. Calder said. "We'll give each team two Aussies, four Yanks, and divide up the rest. Then we're even."

I ended up on a team with Riley's dad and big brother, Logan, Bayani, Daniel, Ty, Deena, and my mom. Logan didn't waste any time coming over to sit by me.

"So. Riley, huh?" he asked.

"What about Riley?"

"You and him. Off together. In the dark."

I bit the inside of my cheek to keep from smiling. He was so jealous, green was practically rolling off him, and not because he's Irish. "You know it," I said, flipping my hair.

You could have knocked him off the log with a sigh. "Seriously?"

"Why? Jealous?"

He hesitated half a beat too long. "No," he said. "Just wondering."

"Wondering what?"

His jaw tightened. "Where you went," he said finally.

"No place special." Okay, I admit it. I was maybe enjoying his worry a little too much. It made me feel good to see him jealous, but I couldn't forget how bad I had felt when I manipulated it the night before. "Seriously. It was nothing," I assured him. "We just went out to the—"

"Pay attention!" Daniel hissed, one finger pressed to his lips. "You're going to miss the clues!"

You learn a lot about people by playing games. Like who's a good sport, and who can be competitive to the point of insanity. Most of the guys on both teams fell into the second category to varying degrees. I kind of expected Logan to be like that; he had something to prove if he thought I had a thing for Riley. Bayani was no surprise, either. I'd played plenty of games with him before, and I knew he didn't like to lose. But Daniel was a revelation. He became our self-appointed team captain, and if he didn't think any of us were giving our best, he was much too happy to chew us out. If I didn't know better, I'd think something more than the game was bothering him. Especially when it was Deena's turn to act out movie titles.

Not that she wasn't great. Our team guessed right away

what movie she had when she pantomimed dancing around and splashing in puddles (*Singin' in the Rain*) or prancing around as she clapped her hands together to mimic a galloping horse (*Monty Python and the Holy Grail*), but the way Daniel was behaving, you'd think she was holding our team back or something.

The score was tied when Deena drew the last slip of paper for the evening. She gave us the signal that meant it was a movie, the word and syllable counts, and then bent down to pick through the rocks at her feet.

"*Rocky!*" Bayani yelled.

Deena shook her head and signaled for us to wait.

"*Rocky Horror Picture Show!*" Ryan tried.

No.

"*Shawshank Redemption!*"

Daniel stared Ty down. "How do you get that?"

"The rocks," he said. "Andy Dufresne collected rocks."

I had no idea what they were talking about, but I gently reminded them how Deena had signaled it was a one-word title, three syllables. They both fell silent.

About then, Deena apparently found the rock she wanted and stood up. She set the rock on the serving table, then spun it like a top.

"What the heck is that supposed to be?" Daniel demanded.

"Uh, she can't talk, D," Logan reminded him.

The rock stopped spinning, and she tried again.

"What's she doing?" Daniel fussed.

"Dunno, mate," Mr. Calder said calmly, "but let's let her give it a fair go, right?"

But the time ran out before anyone could guess.

Deena blew her bangs out of her eyes with a frustrated huff. "The movie was *Inception*," she said. "I was trying to do Cobb's totem."

Another movie I hadn't seen. But apparently Daniel had. "No way we could have guessed it from what you were doing," he sniffed.

"Actually," Bayani said, gripping Daniel's shoulder meaningfully, "the clue was pretty good."

I exchanged a quick look with Logan. Never in all the time I'd known him had I ever seen Daniel act so rude. It was embarrassing. And it was about to get worse.

Daniel shook Bayani's hand off. "She thinks she's so hot because she's the movie freak."

Deena flinched and opened her mouth to snap back at him, but Ty stepped between them, hand clenched at his side. "The term is movie *buff*," he said, his voice like a dog's growl.

"Down boys," Mom said. "You want me to send you both to your rooms?"

The rest of us tried to laugh it off with her, but the whole scene was just so uncomfortable. I felt like I should apologize for Daniel to anyone who would listen, but his rant effectively ended the evening.

Riley came over to sit with Logan and me after the groups split up. "What was *that*?"

I shook my head. "I have no idea. I've never seen him go off on someone like that before."

"He's probably just tired," Logan said.

I watched Daniel stalk toward the corral. "That's probably it."

It's not fair, I texted to Zoe later that night. Deena's been totally nice to Daniel, but he can't stand the sight of her. It's like the green-eyed monster has taken over his body.

What monster? Zoe wrote.

I chuckled to myself. Zoe and I often confused each other with our Greek or American expressions. Talk about having to explain carefully. It's what my gramma calls jealousy—the green-eyed monster.

And Logan? she typed. Does he battle this monster?

I thought about that for a moment. Not sure. I think so.

Sounds dangerous. :)

You have no idea, I texted.

And neither did I.

If anyone remembered Daniel's outburst the next morning, they didn't show it. The mood at breakfast was light. More than a few of us were sore from the roundup, and the best way to deal with the pain was to joke about it.

"You walk like an old man," Logan teased as Bayani sat down—slowly—beside us.

"I might not live to be an old man," Bayani groaned. "I hurt in places I didn't know existed."

"We use a whole set of different muscles while riding a horse," Victoria agreed, "especially in a full chase like yesterday. When we're not used to it . . ." She stretched her legs and winced. "One can only hope the soreness won't last long."

"No kidding." Logan rolled his head from side to side.

It was the first time he even hinted at being stiff. Which probably had a lot to do with the fact that Riley was working in the mess hall that morning and kept passing our table every few minutes, carrying trays or plates or whatever, and was obviously not the least bit affected by the intense ride of the day before. Logan being Logan, he wasn't going to let Riley—or anyone else for that matter—see if he was hurting.

"I was supposed to tell you," Bayani said, "that Liz is waiting for you guys out on the patio to go over today's schedule. So as soon as you're done . . ." He pushed himself up, grimacing as he straightened his back. "I'll see you out there."

"You two go ahead," Victoria told us. "I'll hobble out behind you."

I laughed, even though it hurt my stomach muscles. "Come on," I told her. "We'll hobble out together."

"What a pathetic trio we are," she joked.

Logan bristled at that, but at least he didn't argue about being included in the trio with us. He probably realized it would be pointless, seeing as he had to hold on to the table to steady himself as he tried to stand up.

Pathetic, for sure.

"Oh, there you are," Liz said as we made it to the benches. "I hope you don't mind meeting outside. It's such a lovely morning."

"Spectacular," Victoria agreed, lowering herself gingerly onto the nearest bench.

It was really nice. The morning, I mean. Sunlight angled through the latticework overhead—bright, but not harsh. Warm, but not yet hot. The faint, almost minty, smell of the eucalyptus trees surrounding the patio made the air seem fresh. I could see why so many of the crew had come outside to hang out after breakfast.

"We'd like to take advantage of the milder temperatures this morning and get an early start," Liz told us. "Victoria, if you wouldn't mind taking class time this afternoon . . ."

"Yes, of course," Victoria agreed.

"Very good." Liz signaled to Ty, who hurried over with his case of sound equipment. "We'll go ahead and get you wired while we're talking. Deena has gone back to fetch her kit to get you made up. I've asked Mr. Calder to send the kids over straightaway."

"The kids?" I asked.

"The younger son and daughter," she clarified, as if I should have known. "They're going to walk you two through their daily chores so we can show your viewers what life is like on the ranch."

"Oh." She meant Riley and Rebecca. "Okay, but I thought those chefs were coming up from Melbourne today."

"Yes, of course," Liz said, "to meet with the *When in Rome* group. We may include some clips from their visit in your finished minisodes, but we thought it would be more fun for you and Logan to make the rounds with the kids."

"Great fun," Logan said.

Liz either missed the sarcasm, or she chose to ignore it. "When we're done, we'd like to get some B-roll filler from around the property. Perhaps we could return to that creek, where you went swimming the other day, since we didn't get any footage of that. We'll need to leave enough time for lessons, of course, and then there's your interview with those *Celeb Watch* people this evening."

"We have an interview tonight?" I asked. "I didn't see it on the—"

"Where is he? Where's that stinking rat-faced pig?" Deena stood at the edge of the patio, scanning the groups clustered around various benches.

Ty was running the wire from my lav mic to the receiver at my waist, but he froze at Deena's outburst. "Could you excuse me for a moment? I'll be right back."

He hurried over to talk to her. I could hear the low, urgent tone of his voice, but I couldn't make out the words. His back was to us, so I couldn't read his lips, either. My best guess was that he was trying to calm her down. It didn't work.

She pushed him away. "Get off of me!"

Everyone stopped talking, and a dead silence fell over the patio. Deena marched right up to where Daniel was sitting and waved her makeup kit in his face.

"This is how you want to play? Fine. Bring it. But I swear to you, I will make you cry before this is over."

"Whoa, whoa, whoa." He held up both hands as if to

ward her off. "What the heck are you talking about?"

She slammed the kit onto the bench beside him. "My brushes, Daniel. The foundation primer. The eye color palette. Where are they?"

"How would I know?" he asked. "I have my own kit. What would I want with yours?"

"You tell me. Perhaps so you can do everyone's makeup? Oh, yes, I know you've been whining about how the show doesn't need another makeup artist because you are sooo capable."

"Oh, come on. I never—"

"Save it," she said. "You don't want me here. You've made that clear from the very beginning. But you're *not* going to get rid of me this easily. I am warning you now. Back off."

He stood so that he was looking down on her. "What exactly is your problem? I don't know how you do things in *Hollywood*, but around here we don't go ripping someone's head off without a reason."

I figured it wasn't a good time to point out how that was exactly what he had done to her the night before, so I kept my mouth shut. And anyway, Deena was holding her own. She didn't need help from me.

"Hollywood? Oh, that's right. I've worked with the movies. What's the matter, fat boy? You jealous?"

My lips formed an oooooh, but I didn't dare make the sound. She'd done it now, insulting his physique. Daniel wasn't exactly fat, but he was . . . soft, and sensitive about it.

Liz clapped her hands sharply. "All right. That's enough! You two, over here. Now. Everyone else, let's get to work. Go!" Her lips had tightened, thinning into straight lines until she managed to force them into a smile as she spoke to Logan and me. "Go ahead and finish getting your mics wired," she told us. "I'll be with you in a moment."

Logan looked at me and shrugged. We'd been dismissed.

Travel tip: Australians believe in mateship and a fair go and have strong affection for the underdog, or "battler."

"Bit of drama this morning, I hear," Becca said as she handed me a bucket of chicken feed.

I nodded but couldn't say anything. Not while I was wired. And not with Deena standing fewer than ten feet away, trying to do something with Logan's unruly hair.

Riley wasn't as discreet. "You shoulda seen it. That one with the pink hair"—he nodded toward Deena—"went off like a frog in a sock. I saw her outside the kitchen window. She was seriously cheesed."

"So I heard." Becca lowered her voice. "Dad said she thinks someone broke into her room and stole some of her stuff." She barely bothered to hide her smile as she scattered the gossip along with the chicken feed. She was obviously pleased with herself for scooping her brother. "She thinks that guy Daniel did it. Now everyone's choosing sides and arguing about who's right and who's wrong."

I snuck a quick glance at Ty and Liz. They'd been talking about sequences and camera angles a moment ago, and it looked like they were still at it. Neither one of them had headphones on, so they wouldn't be listening in on the conversation. Or, more importantly, recording it. I couldn't resist speaking up and setting Becca straight. She may have heard about the fight that morning, but I had been there. And I knew both Daniel and Deena better than she ever would. "Deena is missing some of her things," I told her, "but Daniel wouldn't steal anything. He's not like that."

"I dunno," Riley said, "he was a right galah last night."

"He was a what?" I asked.

"A galah. It's a loud, obnoxious bird."

"Oh. Yeah, I guess he was. But that doesn't mean he's a thief. And it seriously was not like him to act like that. Something must have been bothering him."

"Yeah," Becca said, "guilt. I heard some of the guys talking, and they said—"

"Okay," Ty yelled. "We're picking up sound now."

My breath caught in my throat. He'd never warned us before when he was about to record; he said he caught more candid moments if he didn't announce when the camera was rolling. So this must have been a warning for us to stop talking about Daniel if we didn't want our gossip session to end up on tape.

I let my words go, which was probably just as well. I couldn't put a whole thought together anyway—I was too angry. Angry at Becca for being so pleased that Deena and Daniel provided free entertainment, angry at the crew for choosing sides, and angry at Daniel for starting the fight in the first place. What was wrong with everyone?

"Hair looks better," Becca said when Logan returned to us.

"Feels weird," Logan said, gingerly touching his bangs, which had been plastered with hair spray.

"Don't know why they wanted to fix it," Riley said. "Your show's supposed to be reality, right?"

Logan shrugged. "Depends on whose definition of reality we're going with."

"Cut!" Liz yelled. "No self-conscious chitchat. We can't use any of it. Let's see some everyday-activity sort of action instead, shall we? With smiles!"

"Is she for real?" Becca asked.

I sighed. "Completely."

Gramma doesn't have chickens on her farm. She and Grampa used to a long time ago, but she said they were too ornery and messy. Plus, when I was little, one chased me down and pecked at me. So I've been told—I don't remember it clearly. All I know is that I'm petrified of them. That's why I was less than thrilled to get up close and personal with the Calders' chickens when we had to pull the watering trough and the food hopper out of the run to clean them.

"You can wear these," Riley offered, as he handed me a pair of suede work gloves. "They'll protect your hands from the chooks."

"Chooks?"

"Chickens," Becca said, with an eye roll in her voice. "They'll turn on you if they think you're weak, you know." She reached in through the chicken-wire gate and disconnected the water from the trough . . . without gloves. Subtle.

My fists curled tight inside the protection of the leather. I wasn't weak. A tiny bit afraid, yes, but that's not the same thing. I reached for the edge of the trough to help pull it out of the enclosure, but a fat, speckled hen apparently didn't like that I was taking away her water and started to squawk and peck at me. Even though it didn't hurt through the gloves, I yanked my hands away.

Becca gave a long-suffering sigh and nudged me aside. She grabbed hold of the trough and pulled it out herself. A couple of the chickens pecked at her curiously, but when she didn't flinch, they went away.

Riley and Logan pulled out the hopper, and Riley closed the gate.

"Now what?" Logan asked.

"We hose these down and fill 'em back up," Becca said.

I watched the chickens warily as I helped clean out the hopper. They couldn't get at me through the wire mesh, but I swear they were watching me with their beady little eyes.

They probably knew I was afraid of them, just like Becca said. Made sense they wouldn't trust me if they could tell I didn't like them.

I wondered if that was the problem with Daniel and Deena. Daniel clearly didn't like her, and she just as clearly didn't trust him. Could you fix one without fixing the other?

When the hopper was clean, we refilled it with food and slid it into the enclosure. Or, I should say, Becca slid it into the enclosure. I kept a safe distance, standing with Victoria to watch the feeding frenzy begin.

No wonder I was afraid of chickens. They had a singular focus, and that was to get at the food. If another chicken blocked the way, that poor chicken was going to get pecked. What's worse, once other chickens saw it start, they'd join in, pecking and pulling out the feathers of the other bird until it ran away.

"Looks familiar, doesn't it?" Victoria asked.

"Yeah," I said, wondering how she knew about the chicken that chased me when I was little. But then I thought again. Maybe she was talking about how everyone was either jumping on Deena for snapping at Daniel, or jumping on Daniel for stealing from Deena. All it took was that first little peck, and it seemed like everyone was eager to join in. "It's kind of scary."

"Look at that one," she said, pointing to a speckled black hen that had managed to find a portion of a corncob and dragged it away from the trough to eat it. Soon another hen found a piece of cob that was even bigger than the one the first hen had, so the speckled hen abandoned her treasure and pecked at the other hen to get the bigger piece. But as soon as she did that, two more hens swooped in to fight over the piece she had to begin with, so the speckled hen ended up with nothing.

It was all very *Aesop's Fables* for me—it reminded me of the story where the dog lost his bone when he got jealous of his own reflection in the stream. If I didn't know better, I'd think Victoria had planned the whole thing to set up a teaching moment.

"I should get back and help," I told her, and slipped away before she could ask me the moral of the story.

When Liz suggested we spend the day gathering footage of Logan and me doing chores, I don't think she had any clue what she was getting us in for. Riley and Becca moved from one job to the next all morning without even stopping to catch their breath. By the time we were done, I could barely stand. My back ached, and my hands stung from several small blisters.

"Are we through?" Liz asked in a weary voice. The way she draped herself over the fence railing, you'd think she'd been the one doing the chores, not us.

"We're done out here for now," Riley told her, "but if you want a look inside the mess hall kitchen, we'll be starting lunch in just a few minutes."

"No," Liz said quickly. "That's fine. Logan and Cassidy have class time to attend to. Let's call it a wrap."

For part of our lesson, Victoria assigned us some reading about the history of Australia, but I couldn't remember anything that I read. I kept thinking about those chickens. Grampa had told me once that pecking chickens could get vicious. When they kept the birds on their farm, he sometimes had to step in to separate fighting chickens, to prevent them from going at it until one of them was seriously wounded. Or dead. He had to be really careful how he did that, or the chickens might turn on him and he'd be the one who ended up getting hurt.

Is that how it would be if I got in the middle of Daniel's feud with Deena? I couldn't stand to see the way our crew was taking sides. Dividing. But would it help or hurt if I tried to do something about it? What could I even do, anyway?

Finally, Victoria let us go. We hadn't been in class the full three hours, but she must have recognized it was a lost cause. I pulled Logan aside as soon as we were alone.

"I need your help," I told him. "We have to do something about the—"

"Ah, there you are, Cassidy." Liz and her tablet marched toward us. "I was just coming to find you. We have just an hour or so before the interview tonight. Do you think you could take that time to prepare a blog post? We haven't seen one since we arrived."

That's because it's not my blog anymore, I thought. What's the point? But I said, "Sure," and trudged off to my room.

They call Australia the Land Down Under because of where it sits on the globe. To me the name makes sense because of the way so many things are topsy-turvy. The food, the language, the sights, much of it is familiar and unfamiliar at the same time. The official language is English, but you might not know that, listening to people talk. The food comes from all over the world, but with an Australian twist. And the land looks like home, but with eucalyptus and gum trees instead of ash and maple. It really is like being in Oz.

C 13

As it turned out, the *Celeb Speak* crew was late getting to the ranch, so we had plenty of time to get ready. Deena, finding me with an extra half hour to spend in her makeup chair, asked if she could experiment with my hair.

"Nothing outrageous," she said, "but something fun. Braids are making a comeback, you know. How about if we tried something like that?"

"Sure," I said. "Why not?"

Experimenting with hair was something Daniel never had done. In fact, he always told me "natural is your friend," and left it at that. Part of me kept that mantra going in my head while the other part of me was excited to see what

Deena could do. If I didn't like it, I could always have her brush it out.

She combed back a section and divided it into three pieces. "So," she said as she began weaving the sections into a French braid, "what's your favorite place you've ever traveled to for the show?"

Deena kept up a light conversation the entire time she worked on my hair. I couldn't understand how it was that Daniel didn't like her. She was cool. And way nice. And . . . stepping in on what he considered to be his territory. But that wasn't her fault. She was just doing her job.

"There we are," she said, stepping back. "All done."

I turned my head to one side, and then the other. My mirror image did the same. The braid started off center, wrapping around the back of my head and ending in a side-ponytail. "I like it," I told her. "It's simple—"

"—but different," she finished for me. "And, if I don't say so myself, way cute. It looks good on you."

"I like that it's not the same thing everyone else is doing," I told her.

She laughed. "Not yet. You watch, after your interview airs, there'll be girls all over Australia begging their hairdressers to give them a Cassidy 'do."

"Ha. Cassidy 'do sounds like the hair gel my gramma used to use on me: Dippity-do."

"Oh, my gosh. My grandma used that stuff on me, too!

You know, they still make it, right? Different packaging, same product. I got some a while back when I was feeling nostalgic. The smell took me right back to my grandma's pink guest bathroom."

"Uh, excuse me," Logan cut in. "When you birds are done bonding over hair products, they're ready for us."

My stomach went cold. No matter how many times I interviewed, I always got nervous.

"Well, here we go." I slid out of my chair and smoothed the front of my pants before following Logan out of the room.

"Break a leg," Deena called after us. "Or whatever it is you're supposed to do for a TV interview."

"What *are* you supposed to do for a TV interview?" Logan asked.

I shrugged. "Break a leg's a theater thing, but I suppose it works for TV."

"No, I mean for real."

"I don't know. I've never heard of a saying for TV. If TV people aren't as superstitious, I guess you could just say good luck without worrying it will cause something bad to happen."

Logan stopped dead in the middle of the hallway. "No. What I mean is, what do we *do*? I've never done a TV interview before. Are you supposed to look at the camera? Not look at the camera? What if they ask a question you don't know how to answer? What if your answers sound stupid? How are you supposed to—"

"Relax." I took his hand. "You'll do fine."

The interview "stage" had been set up in the main house living room, with a couch angled so that it was facing the upholstered chair opposite, but also facing toward the cameras and the "audience." A couple of umbrella lights were angled to give the set a bright but soft feel.

The camera setup was a lot like when Mom and Dad did their segments—one stationary and one roving. A boom mike hung over the interview pit, even though they had already wired us with lav mics.

To one side of the set, a tall blonde lady in a bright red skirt and killer heels stood with her back to us, talking to a guy I assume was one of her techies. When he motioned that we were behind her, she turned to give us a toothy smile.

"Cassidy. Logan." She reached out her hand to us. "Nicole Sherwood. Pleased to meet you."

Logan mumbled a greeting and shook her hand, but his eyes kept straying over her shoulder to where the stationary camera was set up, and to the chairs beyond where our mini audience—Liz, Deena, his dad, my mom and dad—was sitting. Already, sweat beaded above his eyebrows. He was nervous, which shouldn't have made me smile, but it did. Take away his room of screaming groupies, and Logan lost his swagger.

Well, one of us had to at least *pretend* to be confident. I thought of all those little reminders my mom had been drilling into my head for the past several years and stood a little taller. When it was my turn to greet Ms. Sherwood, I smiled and looked her in the eye, shaking her hand with a firm, confident grip. She nodded, just slightly, but enough that I knew I had connected. Mom always did say that if you "projected confidence," people would respond positively. It looked like she was right.

Ms. Sherwood directed us to the set. "Let's have a seat, shall we?"

She sat in the white chair, and I sat on the couch opposite. Logan sank onto the cushion next to me. He shifted awkwardly and kept rubbing the palms of his hands on his knees like he was trying to wipe something off on his pants. I grabbed one of his hands to stop him, then gave it what was supposed to be an encouraging squeeze. I don't think he took it that way, though, judging by the way he frowned as he looked at my hand on his. I let it drop away.

I would have liked to ask Logan what was wrong, but just then the cameraman gave us the signal, and the interview officially began. Taking a deep breath, I tried to forget everything else and just focus on the three of us.

"Welcome to Australia," Nicole Sherwood said. "I

understand the two of you have already gained quite a following in Oz."

I waited for Logan to respond since, really, the only "following" either of us had seen since we got there were the girls in Mansfield, so I figured the question was his. Especially since Ms. Sherwood was looking right at him. But he didn't say anything. He just stared back at her.

"Oh. Yeah," I said quickly. "It's great knowing we have fans here. Makes us feel right at home."

Ms. Sherwood's focus shifted to me. "And where is it you call home?"

"Ohio," I told her. "My gramma has a farm there, and we stay with her whenever we're not traveling."

"And Logan?"

"Um, I . . ." He stared at the camera and wiped his palms against his pants some more.

"He's from Ireland," I said for him, "but he's been on the road so much lately, home is wherever he sets his suitcase."

"And how did the two of you end up working together?"

Once more, I waited for Logan to answer. I even nudged him with my foot, hoping the cameras wouldn't pick it up.

"My da," he said. And that was it.

I explained about his dad's position with my mom and dad's show. "I guess the network figured that as long as Logan and I were hanging around, we might as well make ourselves useful. Logan didn't want to do the show with me at first, but I was able to convince the network to persuade him. And believe me, my fans are glad I did. They like Logan in the lineup."

The rest of the interview went about the same. After those first few minutes, Ms. Sherwood gave up trying to get Logan to talk and directed all the questions to me instead. Would it be horrible if I admitted that I liked being the one in the spotlight? After answering all those interview questions about Logan, and after having been ignored in town, it felt good to have someone interested in me for a change.

I did try to include Logan in my answers, and I even asked him to chime in a couple of times (which he didn't do), but there was no mistaking it had been my interview.

Even when we were done, Ms. Sherwood had more to say to me than she did to Logan. She thanked us both as they disconnected our mics, but I was the one she told that they'd be airing the interview the next night. And since we wouldn't have access to a television, she told me she'd send the edited interview to us in a digital file.

Logan and I slipped out of the room so Ms. Sherwood could interview my mom and dad next. He was quiet as we walked back toward the bunkhouses. Not good quiet, either. The kind of quiet that builds and builds until you feel like it's going to smother you if you don't do something about it.

"Is everything okay?" I asked. Stupid question.

He didn't answer with words, but the way he looked at

me told me everything was very much not okay.

We walked a little farther, but the silence screamed in my head. So even though I knew better than to keep going, I couldn't help myself. "Is something bothering you?"

He just shook his head. Not helpful.

"Seriously. What's wrong?"

He stopped walking and turned on me so fast I had to take a step back. "Why don't you tell me?"

"Tell you what? I have no idea what you're—"

"If you don't want me doing the shows with you, just tell me. You don't have to try and make me look stupid so we all know how much better you are in front of the camera."

"What?" A chunk of ice grated in my chest. He was angry about the *interview*? After I had just saved his butt from looking like a total idiot?

"You know what," he said.

"No. I really don't."

"'Logan didn't want to do the show with me at first,'" he said in a falsetto voice.

"It's the truth," I said evenly. "You didn't."

"'*I* convinced the network,'" he continued. "'*My* fans like that we added Logan to the lineup.'"

"Well, they do." The ice worked its way down to my stomach. "It was a compliment, Logan. I don't see what—"

"You took over the entire interview."

My mouth dropped open. Seriously? He wanted to go there? "What did you want me to do?" I asked him. "You froze. I had to step in or we would have spent twenty minutes listening to crickets."

"Be honest. You're the minisode diva. I'm just your charity-case sidekick."

I narrowed my eyes. "*I'm* the diva? Give me a break. It wasn't me blowing kisses to my adoring fans in Mansfield."

"I was not blowing kisses. And I did not ask for any of this."

I turned away from him so he couldn't see the angry tears blurring my eyes. *Neither did I, Logan*, I thought bitterly. *Neither did I.*

I tried to sleep, but the Logan in my head wouldn't shut up. "You're a diva," he said. "You took over the interview." I buried my head under my pillow, but all that accomplished was to make it hard to breathe. "I did not ask for any of this," the head-Logan said.

"Aaagh!" I threw the pillow aside. The whole thing was unfair! He was perfectly fine with my being ignored all week, but take the spotlight away from him for just one second . . .

I pulled out my phone to text Zoe, but what would I say? I paced across the room and back, but his taunts followed. Even the twinkle lights I'd draped around the doorway of my room when we arrived couldn't chase Logan's ghost away. Everywhere I turned, there he was.

I couldn't stay in my room any longer. I had to get out. To think. Maybe I couldn't go on a proper walkabout in the bush, but the Calders' property was huge. I could at least walk.

I tiptoed to the door and pressed my ear against the wood, listening for my mom and dad. When I couldn't hear anything, I eased the door open. The bunkhouse was completely dark. Mom and Dad weren't back yet. Good. Then I wouldn't have to sneak.

I let myself out the door and was just about to take the first step down from the porch when I heard voices coming from the side of the bunkhouse. Adult voices. My mom and dad. Bayani. Someone else—Cavin, I assumed. It sounded like they were walking closer. I debated ducking back inside before they saw me, but by then the voices had gotten clear enough for me to understand the words and I wanted to listen.

"The crew is falling apart," Bayani said. "Deena and Daniel can't even be in the same room together. Half the crew's backing up Daniel; the other half's in Deena's camp.

"They'll come around," Mom soothed. "They always do." Only she wasn't fooling me. Her voice was too even, too calm. She was stressing out just like everyone else.

"Well, they'll have to," Bayani said. "We're gonna have a hard time getting this episode in the can if they won't even talk to each other."

"Maybe we should talk to them," Dad suggested.

"Agreed," Cavin said. "This nonsense has gone on long enough. Time for a team meeting."

The four of them faded into the darkness, leaving little puffs of trail dust behind them.

What was wrong with everyone? First Logan and now this? We'd had disagreements among the crew before—we'd been together for so long and in such tight living conditions that we were like a family, and what family doesn't fight once in a while?—but nothing like this. Nothing Cavin and my mom and dad thought they had to monitor. And I didn't even want to think about what was going on with Logan and me. It's like being in the land down under had turned everything upside down.

I had intended to follow my mom and dad. They said they were going to have a team meeting, and I was part of the team. But the closer I got to the crew's bunkhouses, the less I wanted to be a part of the confrontation. I'd had enough of that for one night with Logan.

Problem was, I didn't want to go back to bed, either. What was the use? I wouldn't be able to sleep. I kept on walking past the bunkhouse buildings instead, until I reached the stables. Most of the horses had been moved to the north pasture by then, and those that remained were safely in their stalls for the night. Which meant I had the empty paddock to myself. I climbed onto the fence railing as I had done with Riley the day before and sat, staring into the darkness. The dirt in the paddock had been trampled smooth, except for a few shocks of spiky weeds that poked up here and there. I stared at the weeds, painted in shades of gray by the moonlight, still standing when everything around them had been trampled flat. They stood tall, as if to say that the horses could stomp all they liked, but the weeds would find a way to come back.

Or maybe I was being overly dramatic and looking for hopeful metaphors. Maybe the weeds were just weeds, and the horses would stomp them down tomorrow. Visualizing that didn't help my mood at all.

Sometimes it didn't pay to keep poking back up through the dirt. Sometimes it didn't pay to keep trying. Because sometimes all that effort only made your best friend call you a diva and say you were hogging the spotlight when all you were doing was trying to help.

Australian saying: "The more you know, the less you need."

I heard Malo before I saw him. The night was so quiet, the crunch of his footsteps through the rocky brush was like a sound-effects track—it's all I could hear. I squinted in the darkness until I saw him walking toward the stable, swinging his long stick as he went.

My first instinct was to hide, but that was dumb. If I could see him, I was sure he had seen me. And what was he going to do? Tell my mom and dad? They were busy with the crew. I stayed put and waited for the inevitable.

"Oy!" he called as he got closer. "What you doin' out here so late? And by yourself no less?"

I had an excuse all ready, but there was something about Malo that made him impossible to lie to. My excuse poofed before I could even open my mouth. "The crew is fighting," I blurted out instead.

He leaned against the fence rail next to me, nodding slowly. "So I heard."

"Daniel's phone is missing, and he thinks Deena took it to get back at him for the missing makeup," I told him. Although, odds were if he knew they were fighting, he probably also knew what the fight was about.

Malo took off his hat, scratched his head, then settled the hat back on top of his wiry hair. "The phone is not the problem. Communication between them was already dead."

I thought about my fight with Logan and coughed. "What do we do?" I asked him.

"Communicate." The "duh" tone in his voice was unmistakable.

"I don't know how to get them to do that," I said, "but I feel like I have to do *something*. Our crew family is breaking up. I need to get them back together."

Malo nodded. "You care for them much," he said. "That in itself will work magic. But for now, I should get you back up to your bunkhouse. Morning gonna come right early."

I slid down off the fence. "Thanks, Malo. But I can find my way."

He nodded again, even slower this time. "Yes, Miss Cassidy. I believe you can."

Malo wasn't kidding; morning came way too early. It felt like I had just closed my eyes when Mom tapped on my door and told me it was time to get up.

After I had gotten back from my walk, I couldn't sleep. I tried, but I couldn't stop thinking about Logan, about the crew, about everything. Finally, I gave up and switched on my computer to upload the latest pictures from my phone. At least that would keep my brain occupied.

I sat at the desk for who knows how long, editing the ones I wanted to use for my blog. When I heard Mom and Dad coming through the bunkhouse door, I quickly shut down my computer and slipped into bed before Dad peeked into my room to check on me.

"She's out," he told Mom.

"Good," she said. "The less she knows about this, the better."

"Not something she needs to worry about," Dad agreed as he closed the door. As soon as I heard him walk away, I threw the covers back and crept to the door and pressed my ear against the wood. No good. They must have gone into their own room; their voices were too muffled for me to understand what they were saying. I knew what it was they didn't want me to worry about though, and it was too late.

Ty barely said a word to us as he wired Logan and me for our lavs. Which I guess was fine, seeing as how Logan and I didn't really talk that much, either.

"Mornin'," Logan mumbled at me. Not really *to* me, but in my general direction.

"Good morning," I answered crisply.

And that's pretty much it. I spent another morning watching the sunrise alone. Not that I expected Logan to join me. Not after everything we said the night before. Still, it made me sad.

The rest of the crew didn't appear to be doing much better. Bayani stood with a clipboard, trying to direct everyone where to load the piles of boxes and backpacks, and he may as well have been talking to a bunch of three-year-olds. Half of them acted like they hadn't heard him. The other half shot disdainful looks at the first half and practically threw the stuff into the back of the waiting jeeps, unfortunately missing the part where Bayani was trying to keep it all organized.

Meanwhile, Deena went at my face with her makeup

brushes like she was dot-painting an aboriginal mask. She kept shifting so that her back was always to Daniel, no matter where he stood. Her dance was making me seasick.

Finally, Victoria saved me. "That looks fine," she said, firmly closing the lid on Deena's makeup kit. "Thank you."

Dismissed, Deena gathered her kit in her arms and marched away without even powdering Logan's nose. Not that Logan's nose needed powdering . . .

No. I was not going to think about how cute Logan looked that morning with his tousled hair and sleep-heavy eyes. (Had he stayed up late like I did? Did he feel bad about the way things had gone between us? Could he not sleep?) Didn't matter. I was still mad at him for accusing me of taking over the interview.

Liz showed up just before we were scheduled to leave. She didn't seem to notice that the equipment wasn't all loaded yet. "Well," she chirped, "this will be fun." I couldn't tell if she was being sarcastic or if she was completely oblivious to the mood of the crew.

"Looking forward to it," Victoria said, not quite as chirpily.

Liz gave Victoria a vague smile before turning her attention to me. "Nice choice." She nodded to the khaki shorts I was wearing with my white Marc tee. "The sponsors will be pleased." I didn't remind her that the sponsor-gifted shorts had come with a matching khaki shirt that made me look like I was going on a safari . . . at Animal Kingdom.

Liz looked around. "Where are the Calders?"

I shrugged. "Haven't seen them yet." Which, come to think of it, was kind of weird. They were usually up before the sun, judging by my meeting with Riley that first morning.

"Went back to the main house."

I jumped and swung around. "Jeez, Jack! Don't sneak up on people like that. You almost gave me a heart attack."

"Naw. Little girl like you? Not likely." He smiled, but it didn't quite reach his eyes. Which I supposed was understandable since half the crew was just standing around, and he was stuck with extra work.

"You want a hand?" I offered.

He shifted the box he was carrying and regarded me for a moment. "Now what would your mom say if I let you do that? You're all made up and prettified. Better to let ya stay that way."

There was nothing unkind about the way he said it, but it made me feel like some kind of prima donna standing there doing nothing as he hefted the box into the back of a jeep.

"I'm gonna go check and see if Yans can use some help," Logan said, pointing over to where Bayani stood with his clipboard, looking lost.

"Oh. I could—"

"No. That's okay. I'll go . . . *I'm* not made up."

I bristled. "What's that supposed to mean?"

But Logan didn't answer. He just walked away.

"Well," Liz said in her fake-happy voice. "If you'll excuse me, I'd best check with them to see what's causing the delay." She probably just wanted to escape before it got any more awkward.

Victoria watched the whole thing quietly. She waited until Liz had gone to speak. "Everything quite all right?"

I hugged my arms and raised one shoulder. "I guess."

"That was not very convincing."

"Sorry. I'll put more heart into it next time."

"We're not taping at the moment," she said gently. "If there's anything you need to talk—"

"Small change of plans," Cavin announced.

Cavin walked briskly toward the lineup of jeeps, followed by Liz, Mr. Calder, my mom and dad, and Riley and Rebecca. "Listen up!" he yelled.

The crew stopped what they were doing (even if they hadn't been doing much of anything) and looked to Cavin expectantly. Cavin, in turn, looked to Mr. Calder.

"Right then," Mr. Calder said. "Sorry we're draggin' the chain this morning. Seems Ryan forgot to eat his Weet-Bix today. He's feeling a bit crook, so no bush bashing for him. We're gonna need a step-in who has experience with a fourby."

"I never know what he's talking about," I whispered to Victoria.

"Ryan's sick," Riley answered, "so we need someone else to drive."

"Hey!" I said. "I didn't think we'd see you before we left."

He tipped his hat to me and grinned. "Without Ryan, you're one guide short, so Becca and me are filling in."

"Takes the two of you to make up for one Ryan, huh?" I teased.

"The way he tells it, it does. I think it's more like they couldn't decide which one of us to leave behind, so here I am."

I slid a quick look over to where Logan was standing with Bayani. At least I'd have *someone* along on the trip who was talking to me. "Great," I told Riley. "Which car are you going to ride in?"

He winced. "Sorry. No cars where we're going. All unsealed roads."

"Unpaved," Victoria clarified for me.

"That's why we take *fourbies*, not cars," Riley said.

I folded my arms. "You know what I meant."

My mom caught my eye and signaled for me to be quiet. I nodded and then gave Riley an apologetic shrug. We both turned our attention back to his dad and Cavin.

"With Ryan down, we're short one driver," Mr. Calder said. "And with the other groups here at the Back of Beyond, we can't spare the missus or the hands, so . . . do we have any volunteers?" he asked. "You should be able to handle a stick."

Jack raised his hand. "I can do it."

"Good on ya." Mr. Calder waved him over. "Come let's have a chin wag, and we'll get yer set."

"Everyone else," Cavin said, "get a move on. We should have been long finished loading the equipment and supplies by now. We'll want to get on the road as soon as possible if we're going to reach the camp in time to get set up and be ready to film before the light fades."

Poor Bayani. When it had been him asking for help, half the crew ignored him, but the minute Cavin appeared, suddenly everyone was happy to step up.

If packing up was bad, it was nothing compared to the crew dividing themselves into the waiting jeeps for the ride. You'd have thought we were loading a bunch of kindergarteners the way they scrambled to sit with their friends or, worse, not to sit with someone else. Finally, Bayani threatened that if they were going to spend our time and their energy arguing about seating arrangements, they could stay behind. You could see it about killed him to play the bad guy. Bayani loved to tease me and to dog some of the guys on the crew, but he hated confrontation. His yelling at everyone must have meant he'd had enough.

I was glad we didn't have to worry about arguing over seating arrangements in our jeep, even if Logan and I weren't exactly happy with each other. We didn't really have a choice who rode with us. The minisodes production was separate from *When in Rome*, so it was just Liz, Victoria,

Deena, Ty, Logan, and me. Throw in Malo as our driver, and all our seats were taken care of. Now, if Logan would just talk to me, we'd be set.

The first part of the trip wasn't too bad. While we were still on the paved roads, the ride was smooth. Logan and I had already been wired and powdered (Deena had caught him before we started off), so there was no frantic makeup session in the car—excuse me, jeep—like when we were driving to Mansfield. Liz sat in the front seat, busily tapping away on her tablet, and Malo hummed to himself as he drove. Victoria sat with Logan and me in the middle row of seats so we could work in our class time.

After the Back of Beyond slipped away behind us, Victoria pulled out her bag and handed both Logan and me papers that had a square grid printed on them. Inside each square on the grid was a word or a phrase.

"It's Outback Bingo," she told us proudly. "Every time you can identify and discuss something on your board, you get to cross off the square. The first one to fill the entire board wins."

I eyed the paper suspiciously. "Can't we just fill in a line up, down, diagonal, or across?"

"Consider it full-house bingo. And I'll give you each a head start. Take a look at that." She pointed out the window, but I didn't see anything exciting. Only miles and miles of scrub brush and stubby trees, dissected by a long, weatherworn rail fence. When Logan didn't identify what we were supposed to be seeing, either, she sighed. "Those are grass trees," she said. "Remember? We talked about them just the other day."

Oh, yeah. I saw it now—crooked black trunk; long, spiky leaves that looked like a head full of hair. That is, if someone had really wild hair. Sticking up from the center of the hair were a couple of tall flower spikes. "It looks like something you would see in a Dr. Seuss book," I said.

Victoria smiled at that. "They do have an almost comical appearance, don't they?"

"Absolutely." My pen hovered over the paper. "So . . . does that count as a discussion?"

"Not quite," she said. "Can you remember anything you read about the plant?"

"We were supposed to read about it?" Logan asked.

Victoria sighed and rolled her eyes.

I leaned forward and nudged Malo's shoulder. "You're the local expert. Can you tell us anything about those trees?"

"That's cheating," Logan said.

"It's not cheating," I told him. "It's discussing. Malo?"

His glanced back at Victoria through the rearview mirror, and she nodded her okay. "The yakka is a useful plant to the First People," he said. "The roots are good for eating, the flower nectar makes a sweet drink, the resin a strong glue. The stem of the flower spike can be used for spear fishing, and for making fire."

Okay, I had to admit that was pretty cool. I snapped some pictures of the trees to add to my blog. We played Outback Bingo for the rest of the ride, or the part I was awake for, anyway, and before I knew it, we were pulling to a stop next to another one of the other jeeps. The flat, scrubby landscape was gone, and in its place, hills and rocks and gum trees had sprung up to take its place.

"Are we here?" Logan asked, yawning.

"Not yet," Malo opened his door. "Wait here for a moment." He climbed out of the jeep and walked over to talk to Mr. Calder, who was driving the other jeep.

Liz leaned forward in her seat and peered through the front windshield. "We're in the middle of nowhere," she said, as if we couldn't see that for ourselves. To prove it, she tapped on the screen of her cell phone and then twisted around to show us. "No signal."

Logan twisted around to look out the back window. "Where's Daniel?"

Right on cue, Malo opened the door and slid back into the driver's seat. "The third jeep has fallen behind," he announced. "We're going to circle around to make sure they know which way to go."

"Where are Mom and Dad going?" I asked. Mr. Calder's jeep was bumping over the road ahead, continuing on.

Malo put the jeep in reverse and glanced back over his shoulder to back it up. "They're worried about losing the light before they have a chance to shoot their section."

"Segment," I corrected automatically.

"Yes. That." He cranked the steering wheel, grunting softly from the effort, and then shifted into drive. "They're going to go on ahead and start setting up camp, and we'll meet them there."

"Not as if we have no filming to do," Liz grumbled.

"It won't take long," Malo assured her. "I noticed them behind us just past the billabong near the curve in the road. They can't be too far back."

"Oh. A billabong is on your cards," Victoria told Logan and me. "Do you know what it is?"

Logan raised his hand. "It's where a branch of water flows off from the main source into a sort of dead end."

I checked my card and saw the word there, but I wasn't much interested in fishing out my marker to color it in.

"Who's in the back jeep?" Logan asked.

"Not sure," I told him. There was such chaos when we were supposed to leave that I didn't know who ended up where. Mom and Dad were for sure in the front jeep. And Cavin. And probably Bayani, since he would be manning the camera. Jack was driving the other jeep. Which left Daniel, Becca, and Riley. Probably.

I had no idea how far back the billabong was. I must have fallen asleep before we passed it the first time, because I didn't remember seeing it. I also didn't remember the road being so bad. There were ruts and holes and rocks the size of cantaloupes lying around, and we bounced over them all.

My teeth were rattling by the time we spotted the other jeep, which had stopped smack in the middle of the road.

"Finally!" Daniel said. "Our jeep broke down, and no one even noticed we had stopped."

"Of course we noticed," Victoria said. "Eventually."

He folded his arms. "Oh, that's very nice."

"It's a joke, brother," Malo said, dusting off his hat before he settled it onto his head. "Why don't you show me what's wrong?"

Daniel spread his hands. "How should I know? I wasn't the one driving. And I don't do cars."

"Well," Malo said patiently, "let's have a Captain Cook."

"Huh?"

"A gander. A squiz. A look."

Jack walked up to us, wiping his hands on what probably used to be a white T-shirt. "Already looked. I'm no mechanic, but it looks like the serpentine belt's worn out."

Malo's thick eyebrows rose for an instant. "Show me what you saw," he said, rolling up his sleeves. He and Jack disappeared beneath the hood.

"It was weird," Riley said. "Never felt anything. Never heard anything wrong with the engine. We just all of a sudden stopped."

"So what do you think? The bloke's lying?" Becca shook her head. "Don't be a boofhead. He said the engine stopped, and he was the one driving, not you."

"I'm just saying it was strange, is all."

"Where did the other group go?" Daniel asked.

"They went on to the campsite," I told him. "Malo said they wanted to start shooting while the light was still good."

"Oh," Daniel's eyes strayed beyond us. "They didn't need makeup?"

"Don't worry," Deena said as she walked up beside us. "I'm right here. I didn't steal your job."

"I didn't say you did," Daniel sniffed.

"Oh, really?" Deena shot back, "because I seem to remember you saying—"

"Cassidy, Logan," Victoria cut in, "why don't we explore while we're waiting, and see if we can find any more items on your cards."

"Don't worry," Daniel said. "I'm leaving."

I think he intended a dramatic exit, but since there wasn't really anyplace to go, he ended up stomping five or six feet away from us and sulking on the other side of the broken-down jeep.

"Should I go talk to him?" I asked.

"Perhaps we should give him some time to cool off," Victoria said.

"I don't know." Deena pursed her lips. "He's been on simmer all week. How does your crew put up with it?"

Your crew? The words hit me like a sucker punch. I had always thought of our crew as one big family. Now we had become *our crew, your crew.* Different. Divided.

"Daniel's not usually like this," I said weakly.

"The cards," Victoria reminded Logan and me. "Let's go."

"Don't bother," Deena said, "I'm out." She turned on her heel and walked back to where Ty stood waiting by our jeep.

"Well, that was awkward," Becca said.

Victoria looked defeated. "Perhaps we should see if they need any help." She nodded toward Jack and Malo, still bent over the engine, poking and pointing. It didn't look good, judging by their frowns.

"How far away from a mechanic are we?" I asked Riley.

He shrugged. "We passed the last town on the road a coupla hours ago," he said.

"We don't need a mechanic," Becca said. "Malo usually fixes everything back at the property."

"But that's only when he's got the parts," Riley reminded her. "And his tools."

She chewed on her lip. "We better not be stranded." She marched over to the disabled jeep, as if Jack and Malo needed her to tell them to find and fix the problem. The rest of us followed, because . . . honestly? We were stuck in the middle of nowhere. There was nothing else to do.

Malo was holding a long, thin strip of rubber I assumed used to be the belt Jack had been talking about. "Not a problem to fix," he was saying. "I can get a replacement in town, pick up some tools. Round trip's maybe four, five hours."

"And the campsite is how far up the road?" Jack asked.

"Another hour and a half, maybe two, depending on the condition of the roads," Malo said.

"What are they talking about?" Riley whispered to Becca.

She turned to him, eyes alight. "They're trying to decide what to do with everyone since we have only one working car and are at least two hours to anywhere. Either we take turns riding up to the other campsite, or wait here while Malo grabs the part. If he leaves now, he can get back before dark."

"That sounds good," Riley said. "We won't have to wait too long; Dad'll come back as soon as he sees we're missing."

"Or when their group gets hungry." Becca laughed and elbowed Logan in the ribs. "The food's in the back of your fourby."

"But isn't that the jeep Malo would have to take into town?" he asked.

"We can unload some of the supplies before he goes," I suggested, "and have dinner waiting when he gets back."

"Good plan," Malo said. The three of them had stopped debating and listened to us instead. "Leave it up to the young ones to simplify. Let's pull the food out of the fourby. Takes less petrol to carry less weight."

Half the group pushed the crippled jeep off to the side of the road while the rest of us formed a food-box brigade to pull supplies off the other one. Since Riley and Becca were the only locals among us, Malo pulled them aside before he left.

"Keep everyone together," he told them. "Find the box with the torches and have 'em ready before it gets dark. Set up chairs away from the grass to avoid the nasties."

"We know; we've been camping before," Becca told him. "Just hurry up and go, so you can get back."

Australian saying: "May as well be *here we are* as *where we are.*"

Malo hadn't been gone more than twenty minutes when the murmuring started. And part of that, I have to admit, was my fault.

While Daniel, Jack, and Victoria started setting up the grills, Becca gathered Logan, Riley, and me one by one and told us in a low voice to meet her behind the jeep.

Riley frowned at her. "Becca, what—"

"Behind the fourby," she said.

I couldn't decide whether to be intrigued or irritated. Whatever she had planned, Becca was obviously very pleased with herself. But at the same time, she kept checking over her shoulder to make sure no one else tried to join in our conversation. Well, if Riley and Logan were going to play along, I figured I might as well, too. At least she included me in her drama. I had to admit that was worth something.

Once we were all safely cloistered behind the jeep, she looked at us in turn, not quite smiling, but with a definite gleam in her eye. "It wasn't an accident," she announced.

"What wasn't an accident?" Riley asked.

"The car breaking down. I overheard Malo tell that guy Jack that"—she paused to check over both shoulders—"the belt didn't wear out. It was cut."

"Why would someone cut the belt?"

I asked. Too loudly. Talk about all activity coming to a screeching halt. I just turned everyone into a bunch of gawking statues.

Deena was the first one to recover and came racing around the side of the jeep. "You think someone cut that part on purpose? How do you know?"

"Who would do that?" Ty asked.

"Gee," Daniel said, staring pointedly at Deena, "I wonder who might not want me to make it in time for the shoot tonight. Let me think."

"For sure, Daniel," Ty snapped, "because it's all about you."

"For all we know," Deena said, "you cut it yourself so you could bask in the drama."

Jack stepped in front of Daniel, folding his arms across his broad chest. "You're the outsiders," he said, staring Ty and Deena down. "If I had to start assigning blame, I'd be looking at you."

"Nice going, you drongo," Becca said to me. "Ever wonder why I was trying to tell you guys in *private*?"

"Oh, belt up," Riley said. "She didn't mean for everyone to hear."

"How about we cook some dinner?" Victoria said a little too brightly.

Deena's lip curled. "Give it a rest."

"Stop!" Liz finally spoke up like she was coming out of a coma. "One more word from any of you and you're fired, do you understand?"

That stopped the volley of words, but it didn't touch the deadly looks being shot back and forth. Which is why I kept my eyes to the ground. Becca was right: I was an idiot for having opened my big mouth. It's not as if things weren't bad enough already. Now the crew was fighting even worse, slinging accusations. It was my fault. And I had to fix it.

But before I could even begin to think of a plan, Liz started handing out orders. "You," she barked, pointing at Jack, "help the boys get some chairs set up so we'll have someplace to sit. And you two"—she pointed to Becca and me—"help Victoria go through those food boxes. Maybe we'll all feel better after we eat. Go!"

I have to say this for her, when Liz wanted to take charge, she took charge. Everyone jumped, following her orders. Except Ty and Deena. Liz called them over to have a "chat" with her, and it was clear by the way her jaw clenched that the talk wasn't going to be pleasant.

"Why'd they get singled out?" Becca asked.

"Don't worry," I told her. "I'm pretty sure each one of us is going to get a turn."

On short notice, I think we did a decent job with the dinner. In the supply boxes, we found steaks and foil-wrapped potatoes to put on the grill, and Anzac biscuits for dessert. The biscuits were like oatmeal cookies with coconut in them, and they were really good.

Maybe Liz was right; maybe we were all cranky because we were hungry. After everyone had been fed, you could feel some of the tension melt away. It almost felt like we were back to normal—until the sun went down.

I'm guessing we had been stranded for more than five hours by that point. It's hard to know for sure because I hadn't paid attention to what time it was when we turned back to look for the third jeep. But it *felt* like five hours. We'd had time to check under the hood, formulate a plan, unpack one jeep, have a huge argument, set up a sort of camp, make and eat dinner, and clean up afterward. A lot had happened. But the passing of time didn't register so starkly until it got dark.

It's weird how going from daytime into night can alter your perspective. Now it felt like we'd been waiting around *all day*. I started to feel small and trapped as the darkness closed in. And I knew for a fact that too much time had passed. Malo should have returned by now.

Which is another reason why I'm guessing it had been at least five hours. Malo said it would take him only four to make it in to town and back. He expected to be able to replace the broken belt while it was still light.

"I wonder what happened," Deena said as she stared at the glowing coals in the barbecue grill. Several of us had gathered around the grill to stay warm because the temperature had dropped along with the sun.

"Who says anything happened?" Becca asked.

"It's been so long," Deena said.

"He could have miscalculated how far we'd come since we passed that town," Logan offered. "Maybe it's taking longer than he thought it would."

"Or maybe he couldn't find his way back in the dark," Ty suggested.

Riley shook his head. "No way. Malo knows these roads like he knows the lines on his own face. And if he did get lost, he'd navigate by the stars. Don't worry. He's coming."

"What I find odd," Daniel said quietly, "is that our host hasn't come looking for us."

Deena stiffened. I'm guessing she didn't see Daniel come up and join us by the grill. She shifted from foot to foot uncomfortably, but what was she going to do? Tell him to go away? Not when the night was going from cool to cold and the only warm spot was where we were standing.

"Daniel's right," Jack said. "Unless he figured his man Malo could handle it, so he'd just wait until the crisis was resolved."

Becca stared at him hard. "What do you mean by that?"

"You heard what Malo said," Jack answered. "The camp is only an hour and a half away. When we didn't show up, he had to know something was wrong. Why didn't he come back to see what it was?"

"Probably because he had to wait around so someone could 'film while the light was good,'" she shot back. Her voice changed as she said that last bit, mimicking what she'd heard Liz say and making it sound shameful.

"He'll be here," Riley said. "It hasn't been dark that long. If they were busy trying to catch the light, he only just got the chance to slip away."

"How can you know?" Logan challenged. I guess he didn't like the insinuation that the filming had been more important than coming to see where we were, either. His dad was the producer, after all.

"How cold does it get at night?" Deena asked. "They've

got all the tents, you know. We could freeze out here, exposed to the elements."

"No one is going to freeze," Victoria said firmly. Even her voice held a touch of irritation.

Daniel eyed Deena and smirked. "Not from the air temperature, anyway."

On it went. The accusations began all over again. Lines drawn. Sides chosen. And I'd had enough. I eased out of the warmth—and the chill—of the circle.

I marched off to the pile of backpacks to find my hoodie, swiping at the tears that blurred my vision. The wanderer part of me loved Australia. That part of me loved the ruggedness of the high country, the wildness of the bush. It loved that there were plants and animals down under that you wouldn't see anywhere else on Earth. But another part of me wished we'd never come. What should have been a fun trip together had turned into a wedge, splitting us apart.

Even in my hoodie, I shivered as I watched the others argue. It was not how this campout was supposed to go. Wandering over to the jeep, I sank down to sit on the bumper and hugged myself, feeling very much alone.

Then I heard Logan's voice. "Hold on, I want to grab a sweatshirt, too. I'm freezing."

It's stupid, now that I look back on it, but I thought he was talking to me. How could he have been, though, when I'd been hiding on the other side of the jeep where he couldn't see me? Still, I stood up, relieved. We might argue once in a while. We might be mad at each other. But when it came right down to it, we were best friends. We would always be there for—

"I'm telling ya, mate. Yanks are all alike." Becca. Great. "But this one . . ." She whistled.

"She's not that bad," Logan said. "A little dramatic, maybe."

Becca laughed. "A little?"

"Okay, so she's theatrical. What do you expect? Look at where she comes from. It's in her blood."

"She makes me crazy," Becca said, shuddering.

Logan pulled his hoodie on over his head. His voice was muffled as he answered, but it was clear enough for the words to hit me right in the stomach. "Be happy you don't have to work with her."

My stomach tumbled. It shouldn't have surprised me to hear Logan say that after our argument the night before, but it still stung. Worse than that, though, was the tiny voice inside me that said he might be right. Maybe I could be a little dramatic. But what was I supposed to do about it? Like he said, it was "in my blood."

I stepped around the end of the jeep so Logan could see me. "Sorry to be such a burden to you."

"Cass? Where did you go? I was looking for—"

"Right, Logan," I snapped. "I heard what you said to Becca."

He frowned. "You were eavesdropping?"

"Don't change the subject."

"What subject?" He looked to Becca, and she shrugged, so he turned back to me. "What are you talking about?"

"If you don't want to work with me, you should say it to my face."

"What?" And then the realization showed in his face. "No. You got it wrong. I wasn't talking about you."

"Come on, Logan." I clenched my hands at my sides. "I'm so dramatic. I have it in my blood. I heard y—"

He threw up his hands. "Have it your way. You'll believe what you want to believe."

"I'll believe what I heard."

"Fine."

"Fine!"

I would have liked to march away from him then, if it wasn't for the little problem of being stranded with no place to go. But I couldn't just stand there, either. I could already feel hot, angry tears forming, and there was no way I was going to let him see me cry. So I turned on my heel and walked away from Logan and Becca, head high, back straight, even though I felt like curling up in a ball somewhere.

Once the shadows swallowed me up, I ducked behind a tree, despair swirling around me like a heavy black cloud. Which only served to prove Logan's point that I was overly dramatic. And that made me feel even worse. I wanted to go back and tell Logan I was sorry. And I would, as soon as my eyes stopped stinging and my chest didn't feel so tight. Until then, all I wanted was to get as far away from him as I could. Wrapping my arms around myself, I trudged deeper into the trees.

Which turned out to be not such a great idea.

If I thought walking away was going
to be easy, I was wrong. First, the ground was really rocky
and uneven. Second, the tree branches overhead were so
thick that the watery moonlight couldn't get through. It
was dark, and I couldn't see where I was going. Worse, thin
little pine branches stuck out at face level and I kept walking into them. I could just imagine the look I'd get from Liz
when she saw the scratches. Deena would have some work
to do before we could film any more segments. *If* we filmed
any more segments. Hard to imagine how we would when
Logan clearly didn't want to work with me and everyone
else was fighting.

If only we could get back to the ranch. Work things
through. Start over. Then everything would be better. I was

sure of it. Or at least I hoped it could happen that way.

After a while, the trees became smaller and farther apart. Up ahead, the ground began to slope upward. I was about to change direction to save myself the climb when I had an idea. Back in Costa Rica, when the Internet was down at the farm, Logan and I had been able to find a signal by standing at a certain spot on the hillside. Maybe if I climbed this hill, I could find a cell signal and call for help.

The climb turned out to be more like a hike. I quickly discovered that my sponsor-gifted shoes were not made for hiking around rocky hills. The soles were thin, so the bottoms of my feet felt every bump and piece of rock. Plus the traction wasn't good, so I kept slipping, falling two steps back for each step forward. But I was determined. Finding a signal would solve everything. At least that's what I kept telling myself. I climbed all over that hillside, searching, waving my phone this way and that, until I was too tired to go on.

And cold. Summer or not, once the sun had gone down, the temperatures dropped quickly. I shivered as I picked my way back down the hill. It probably hadn't been a very smart idea to walk away from "camp" without putting on long pants. Like Victoria said, I probably wouldn't freeze or anything, but as much as I hated to do it, I had to return to camp.

I trudged back into the woods. It was slow going since I couldn't really see. Which is probably why the trees seemed to go on forever. The walk was much longer than I remembered on my way to the hill, anyway.

Which should have been a clue.

When I reached the edge of the woods, I drew up short. The roadside where the camp should be was empty. No disabled jeep. No barbecue grill. No arguing family of crew members. Nothing. Where had they gone? Maybe Malo had gotten back with the replacement part while I was off in the woods, fixed the jeep, and they were gone. But they wouldn't have left me behind.

Would they?

They might if they didn't know I was missing. No one was communicating. Each group could have thought I was riding with the other one. What if they didn't realize their mistake until they got to the campground, an hour and a half away? It would take them another hour and a half to come back, and all I could do was wait for them, cold and alone.

I panicked for a couple seconds before I noticed that the road had changed in my absence. It had gotten narrower, with scrub crowding in on it from both sides. A deep rut cut along one section where no rut had been before. And then it finally dawned on me. This was a different section of road.

I must have gotten turned around after I came down from that hill and lost my way in the woods.

Looking back at the trees, I considered trying to retrace

my steps to the ridge and then setting out for the camp once more, but I'd already lost my way once. What if I got even more lost by trying again? At least I had found the road. I could just follow it until I came to the camp.

Except I didn't know which way to go, up the road or down. If I walked the wrong way, I'd be getting farther away from where I wanted to be, not closer. I hugged my arms tight and tried to think of what to do.

Once I had gotten separated from my mom and dad at a street market in Marrakesh. It was hot, and dusty, and crowded with people and dogs and carts and motor scooters that were so noisy you could barely hear your own voice. I'd been right next to my mom until I paused at a booth to look at some charms. I told her I wanted to stop, but she must not have heard me. When I turned around, I couldn't see her anywhere. Mom and Dad had always said that if I got lost, I should stay where I was and that they would come and find me. So I stayed. It took them a few minutes, but they did come looking for me.

The thing was, back then they knew where to look. Now no one knew where I was. Even if I stayed put, how would anyone find me? The way I saw it, I didn't have any choice but to try to find my way back through the woods.

Bad call.

Australian saying: "Keep your eyes on the sun and you will not see the shadows . . . unless it is nighttime."

It shouldn't have happened. I'd walked into the trees that night twice before, so I knew the ground was uneven. Because of that, I was being extra careful, taking it slowly even though the dark and the cold and the scratchy branches made me want to hurry. I even stopped every few steps to listen, hoping to hear voices, movement, anything that would tell me I was getting closer to camp. So it's not like I was dashing carelessly through the woods when I fell.

Have you ever had one of those dreams where you're running, and all of a sudden there's no ground beneath you, and you jerk awake with a sensation of falling? That's what it was like. Except instead of running, I was walking. And instead of jerking awake, I fell and landed hard on my hands and knees. I didn't even realize I was hurt until I tried to get up. Even then, I was more confused than hurt. Why wouldn't my leg hold me up? And then, like a late-breaking wave, the pain hit me.

I rolled over so I could sit up, rocks and pine needles poking through the seat of my shorts. In the tiny spots of moonlight that fought their way through the mesh of branches overhead, I could just make out the gash on my knee. Now that the pain had registered, it throbbed to the beat of my jackrabbit pulse. Not just in my knee, but also in the palms of my hands. I took a deep breath and let it out with a shudder.

Along with the pain, fear rolled over me again and again. I was lost. I was hurt. No one knew where I was. Suddenly, that moment back at camp when I thought I was on my own was nothing. Now I *really* felt alone. Desperate. Afraid.

I fought back the tears. Not that there was anyone around to hide them from, but I was afraid that if I started to cry, I would never be able to stop. What a mess I'd made of things. It wasn't bad enough that I had picked a fight with my best friend. Oh, no. I had to make it worse by storming off. Now I'd probably never get a chance to tell him I was sorry. Yes, I was still mad at him for what he'd said, but I had said some mean things, too. What if those were the last words he ever heard from me?

No. That way of thinking was plain stupid. I was being a drama queen, just like he said. I wasn't going to die from a scraped knee. Or the cold. Or starvation. Or the wild animals in the bush. Okay, so I hadn't seen any wild animals so far, but I was starting to be aware of the noises around me. The rustling of leaves, a snapped twig here, a slither of movement there. I just hoped they'd keep their distance.

And I decided I wasn't going to just sit there being afraid. I scooted forward—not an easy feat with those rocks scraping the backs of my thighs and my hands stinging with the effort—so that I could use the trunk of the nearest tree to pull myself up. I still had no idea where I was or what I was going to do, but at least when I was standing, I didn't feel as helpless as I had sitting on the ground.

I tried again to put weight on my injured leg and I found that I could, but not much. My knee throbbed. And since there was no way it was going to let me walk, I hopped to the next tree, leaving one trunk to grab the next. And then another. And then my foot landed wrong on the uneven ground and rolled under my weight. Icy hot, electric pain zapped through my ankle, and I just about fell again.

I didn't even care if I cried anymore. My breath caught in a sob as I braced myself against the tree trunk, its bark rough and dry against my cheek. It took all the courage I had to keep going. I made myself take a step.

"Aaagh!"

Nope. It wasn't going to work. My ankle and knee could barely hold me up, let alone allow me to walk. I may not have a choice but to stay still until someone came to find me.

I was starting to sink into the pit of feeling sorry for myself again, but then I heard a voice, calling out. I thought I must have imagined it at first. Wishful thinking and all that. But then I heard it again. I wasn't sure what it said, but I do know that I've never been happier to hear another person's voice. "Coo-ee!" it called once more.

I could have melted from relief. I cupped my hands around my mouth and called back, "Coo-ee!"

The answer was quick and definitely to my left. "Coo-ee!"

I repeated the call, "Coo-ee!"

The reply came back much closer. And then Malo appeared, walking out of the trees like a living shadow. "Miss Cassidy," he said, like he wasn't surprised to see me at all. "Lots of people looking for you."

Swiping a tear from my cheek, I told him lamely, "I got lost."

"I see." He looked me up and down and shook his head. "You do seem to enjoy wandering off by yourself."

"I wasn't going to go far," I said, "just far enough. But when I tried to go back, I lost my way and . . ."

"Yup. You did. You're quite a ways off." He propped his stick against a tree and bent to look at my knee. "Gonna need to clean this up, for dead cert." I hissed in a breath as his finger brushed the skin next to the gash. He stood and patted me on the arm. "She'll be all right. Messy, but superficial. Can you walk on it?"

I shook my head. "I hurt the other ankle, too."

"Well, that does present a bit of a Harry Lime."

"A what?"

He smiled, his teeth white in the darkness. "Trouble," he said. "Complication."

"I'm sorry," I said in a small voice.

"Naw, you're not to be feeling bad about that. It just means it could be slow going, gettin' you out of here." He pushed back his hat and scratched his head, looking around as if he could find a solution hiding in the dark. "Not as burly as I once was, or I could carry you."

"You said others were looking for me, too?" I asked hopefully. I wouldn't have minded too much if Logan showed up to help carry me back to camp.

"We split up," Malo said, shrugging. In other words, however many people went looking for me had gone in different directions.

I felt bad all over again for causing so much trouble. And I guessed I'd feel even worse after my mom and dad got through with me. Everyone was probably ready to move on to the real camp, but since I'd run off, they'd had to wait for me. It wouldn't be the first time Mom and Dad had lectured me about going off on my own. I knew from experience that it wouldn't be pretty.

"How long ago did you get back?" I asked Malo, half dreading the answer.

"Not long," he said. "Arrived to find Miss Victoria and the others frantic that you were gone."

Guilt twisted inside, and I pressed my hand to my stomach to stop it. "I thought you'd get back sooner," I told Malo. "Are we farther from town than you thought?"

He shook his head. "Jeep broke down on the way. Reckoned it was closer to walk back here than to keep on in that direction."

I forgot all about my ankle, my knee, and the coil in my stomach. "What? Yours broke down, too?"

"I believe the belt went out," he said calmly. "Couldn't see well enough in the dark to get a good look at it."

"Like the other jeep?" I asked. "That's kind of unusual, isn't it?"

"Yes, Miss Cassidy," Malo said. "Yes, it is."

He didn't say anything more, but he didn't have to. I could put the pieces together. Two broken-down jeeps was way too coincidental. Riley's dad didn't seem like the kind of guy who would let the maintenance on his jeeps slide to the point where one would break down, let alone two. Someone had messed with them. But who? And why?

"Tell you what," Malo said. "You lean on me."

"What?" I blinked, and my conspiracy theories evaporated.

Malo handed me his walking stick. "Use this on the one side for support. I'll prop you up on the other side. Let's give it a burl and see if we can't make it back."

I did as he said and took a tentative step. It wasn't as bad with him there to hold me up. We hobbled along in silence. (Okay, I hobbled; he walked.) I wondered if maybe he would ask why I left the camp or what I needed to think about, but he didn't. In fact, he didn't say anything. Still, there was something about him that made me want to spill everything.

"You're probably wondering why I walked away from camp," I said.

"Watch your step." He helped me over a bump on the ground.

"I had an argument with Logan," I told him. "No, really, it started earlier than that."

Malo listened without interrupting as I poured out the entire story from that first night I left Logan standing with Riley until the fight by the jeep. When I was done all he said was, "I see."

And then I felt really stupid. I mean, what had I expected him to say? It's not like he could fix what had happened any more than I could.

We walked a little farther in silence, and then when I

had to stop and rest, Malo crouched down beside me. He stared into the darkness for a few minutes, and then he cocked his head to look at me.

"You know, my people have a story about a man who went on a walkabout to contemplate his life. He learned many things on his journey, but he began to be lonely. Like you."

I dropped my gaze to the rock I was sitting on. How did he know that? I hadn't said anything to him about how alone I felt.

"One day," Malo continued, "the man found a small dingo pup, curled into a ball and sleeping in the shade of a large rock.

"This man knew that wild dogs can be dangerous; but the pup was so small, and he looked harmless. The man took the pup and tucked it close to his heart and carried it with him on his journey. The pup scratched and bit, because that is what dingoes do, but still the man would not let it go.

"As the days went by, the pup grew larger. It grew and grew until its bites and scratches became too much for the man to bear. The man dropped to his knees, but still he held on to that dingo. Finally, as he lay wounded and weary, the man realized he would never be well again until he let the dingo go."

Malo paused and looked at me, then off into the darkness again. "Jealousy is like that wild dingo," he said softly. "It will always bite the one who carries it."

I was glad Malo had looked away so he wouldn't see me wipe the tears from my eyes. I thought of the harm my own jealousy had caused to my relationship with Logan. How it made Becca bitter. How it was eating Daniel alive. "Sometimes it's hard not to pick up the pup," I told Malo.

He glanced at me and nodded, a smile touching on his lips. "Celebrate your friends' accomplishments," he told me. "Their successes do not take away from your own. Let joy be the animal you hold close to your heart."

19

The more I walked on it, the less my

ankle hurt, which is weird when you think about it. But I guess that's what "walking it off" means. I wished my knee would do the same, but it seemed to be absorbing all the pain that was leaving my ankle.

Malo didn't even hesitate as we pushed our way through the shadows and the low-hanging branches. Riley had said that Malo had lived there his entire life; he probably knew the area like his own hand. I almost cried when I saw the faint light up ahead, smelled the smoke from the grill, heard voices.

You'd think I had been gone for days instead of hours, the way Victoria fussed over me when she saw me.

"Oh, my goodness! Cassidy!" She ran over and wrapped her arms around me, squeezing me so tight I could barely breathe. You'd have to know Victoria to realize how unusual that is. She's proud of her British restraint and doesn't like to show emotion. But I swear I could hear a tremble in her voice as she demanded, "Where have you been?"

"I just needed to—"

But she didn't wait for an answer. She held me at arm's length and *tsked* over the twigs in my hair and the dirt on my clothes. And then she saw my knee. "What have you done to yourself?" Suddenly, she was all business again. She ordered Deena to go grab the first-aid kit, and led me to one of the folding camp chairs.

I sat obediently, because honestly? When Victoria gets like that, you don't question, you just *do*. She started digging through the kit Deena gave her, and I looked around until I saw Logan standing off to the side of where everyone had gathered to gawk at Victoria fixing my knee.

He looked miserable, which would have given me some satisfaction just a few hours ago, but now it made me feel awful. I kept staring at him, trying to get him to look at me, but he wouldn't.

Then Victoria swabbed the cut with an alcohol pad, and I'm sorry to say I forgot all about Logan. The sting literally took my breath away. I squirmed to escape it, but she gripped my leg. "Don't move," she ordered. "We're almost done. The wound needs to be clean or you run the risk of infection."

I bit my lip and nodded, holding my breath until she finished. Finally, she covered the cut with a bandage, and I let the breath out with a sigh.

"Now," she said, "let's have a look at your hands."

She unwrapped another alcohol pad. I had to look away when she bent to her work.

Deena patted my shoulder. "You really did a number on yourself. Good thing you didn't land on your face. I don't know how I would have covered that."

She laughed, and I laughed with her. Just wait until she saw my face in the light. It was probably pretty scratched up from all those branches. At least she was being sympathetic. I should probably enjoy it while I could; my mom and dad probably wouldn't be quite so understanding.

Speaking of . . . I looked around, but I didn't see them anywhere. "Where are my mom and dad? Are they out looking for me?"

Deena shook her head. "Haven't seen them."

I twisted in my seat to look up at her. "Since I got back?"

"Since we split from them this afternoon."

That was weird. By now they would have realized something was wrong when we didn't meet them at the campsite. So what was stopping them from coming back to see what was—

Oh.

Two jeeps were down. Whoever cut the timing belt on the one probably messed with the belt on the other. And that someone could have also sabotaged the third. Maybe my mom and dad were stuck at their camp the same way we were stuck where we were.

It might sound paranoid, all this talk about sabotage, but something similar had happened when we were in Costa Rica. One of our own crew members had disabled the Internet at our lodge so we wouldn't realize they were hacking into my blog and posting mean messages.

Someone was messing with us again. And I had a pretty good idea who was behind it. It had to be Mom and Dad's rival show, *A Foreign Affair*. They'd sent people to mess with *When in Rome* in the past; of course they'd do it again. We'd never been able prove it was *A Foreign Affair*—even when one of the hired saboteurs had confessed—but I didn't doubt it for a minute.

But who could they have gotten to get to us in Australia?

The one who sabotaged us in Costa Rica had been a new crew member. I stiffened and glanced at Deena's hand on my shoulder. She was new. So was Ty. *A Foreign Affair* wouldn't be so obvious as to go through the crew again . . . would they?

But who else could it be? Malo? Mr. Calder? That didn't make sense.

I eased forward in my chair until Deena's hand dropped away. "Thanks, Victoria," I said. "I, uh . . . I'm going to go say hi to Logan now."

"Oh. Well." Victoria sat back on her heels. "All right, then. I'm pleased you're feeling better."

"Good idea," Deena said. "He's been worried about you all evening."

She smiled down at me like she was sharing a secret. Not a bad secret, either, but something fun and hopeful. She gestured with her eyes to where Logan stood, looking as if he'd swallowed a bug. "Go," she mouthed.

Okay, so maybe it wasn't her. I couldn't believe she'd be so cool and understanding while plotting against the show. Ty, then. Maybe. I didn't know. *Someone* was messing with us, I was sure of it. And I was going to find out who it was.

I must have looked pathetic, hobbling over to talk to Logan. When he saw me coming, he rushed over to meet me.

"I'm sorry, Cass," he said, just as I was saying, "I'm sorry, Logan."

"I wasn't talking about you before," he said. "I swear. But . . . I shouldn't have been talking about Deena, either. If you hadn't overheard—"

"I shouldn't have gotten mad," I told him. "And . . . wait. You were talking about *Deena*?" Things were worse than I thought if Logan was choosing sides like everyone else. I pulled him over to the other side of the jeep. Not exactly private, but it would have to do.

"I need to apologize," I told him.

"No," he said quickly. "I got mad, too."

I shook my head. "Not just for tonight. All week. I've ... been jealous. It's changed the way I've acted around you, and that wasn't fair."

"Jealous? Of me?" Logan laughed. "You're kidding, right?"

"No. I'm serious. I watched you get all the screaming fans and the followers online and the questions from the magazine, and I felt left out."

"Wow." His smile faded, and he looked at me with the most serious expression I've seen on him since ... ever. "You can't be jealous of me. I'm jealous of you."

"No way," I told him. "For what? You're the one with all the fans."

"Only because Liz knows how to manipulate the public. You know she tipped off those groupies in Mansfield, right?"

I remembered how she had whipped out her phone as soon as she spotted those first two girls. "You're kidding."

"Nope. I felt like a real loser when I figured it out. Here I was thinking I was some big star with hundreds of fans, and she set the whole thing up."

"You do have hundreds of fans. Probably thousands. All she did was tell them where to find you."

"It was still fake," he said. "But you ... you're genuine. And the way you handled that interview ... I choked, but then you made it look easy. I shouldn't have snapped your head off about it."

I could feel the heat rising in my face, and I looked away so he wouldn't see me blush. It felt good to hear him say that. Not the part where he said he was wrong, but that I did okay. It meant a lot to me. "So I guess we're even," I said. "Maybe now's a good time to call a truce."

I stuck out my hand so we could shake on it, but he shook his head. "We can do better than that." He pulled me into a hug and all the bad feelings from the week faded away. I settled my cheek against his chest, breathing in the smell of clean cotton and Logan. For the first time since we arrived in Melbourne, I was completely content.

Well, almost.

"Logan . . ." I had to clear my throat because my voice was shaking so badly. "I've been wanting to tell you something all week, and . . ."

Wouldn't you know that Becca would walk around the corner of the jeep just then? She took one look at Logan and me hugging and threw up her arm to shield her eyes. "Hey, none of that!"

I pulled back reluctantly. There would be more hugging later (I hoped), but for now, there was something else I had to do. "Becca," I said, "can you go get Riley? We need to talk."

Travel tip: It may seem strange for a society that was founded by convicts, but Australians value honesty.

There's nothing like a good conspiracy theory to bring friends together. After your friends are done thinking you're crazy, that is. I told Logan, Riley, and Becca what I'd concluded about the jeeps and Daniel's cell phone and Deena's makeup kit. They didn't say much, but they exchanged all sorts of raised-eyebrow glances.

"When you fell, did you hit your head?" Becca asked.

"Becks!" Riley said in a low voice, elbowing her.

"What?" she challenged. "You blokes were thinking the same thing. Admit it."

"Was not," he said quickly. "Not exactly, anyway." He looked to me apologetically. "You got to admit, it does sound like you're a few palings short of a fence."

"No," Logan said. "She may be right. You shoulda seen what happened in Costa Rica. Crazy stuff."

"So what do you want us to do about it?" Becca folded her arms, challenging as usual, but I could tell she was in by the way her eyes lit up.

"We," I said, looking at each one of them in turn, "are going to find out who's doing this. Eventually, whoever it is is going to do something to give themselves away."

"You're assuming the person is here with us now," Logan said, "but what if it's someone back at the property?"

Riley shook his head. "No way. Only ones there are Mum and Ryan and half a dozen station hands who've been with us forever. None of 'em would do anything like what you're talking about."

"If someone has truly been working against you," Becca said, "what makes you think they'll give themselves away?"

"They always do," I told her. "We just have to keep our eyes open."

The crew slept together that night. It was too cold to hold on to grudges. We made beds on the ground, with disposable tablecloths for blankets and backpacks for pillows, and huddled as close as personal space would allow. The guys even volunteered to take the outside spots. Victoria, who I always thought of as a very private person, actually seemed to be okay with the sleeping arrangements.

"Think of it, Cassidy," she whispered when I asked her about it. "We began the evening as a family divided. But when you were lost, everyone put aside their differences and worked together to find you. Now look at us. Relying on each other again. Protecting each other again. I do believe our family is back."

She snaked an arm around my waist and drifted to sleep. I smiled in the darkness. Well, what do you know? I may have actually helped to end the crew division after all. Not exactly how I'd planned, but I'd take it. I closed my eyes, warm and happy, in spite of the cold.

"Cass. Psst. Cass." A voice pulled on the edges of my dream, snagging the loose threads, unraveling the sleep. It was still dark outside when I woke up. I shivered and started to pull the tablecloth tighter around me when a hand touched my arm.

I almost screamed but the voice said quickly, "Shh. Cass, it's me."

"Logan? What . . . ?"

"Shhh," he said again. "I want to show you something."

I slid out from under Victoria's arm and sat up as quietly as I could (which is no small trick when you're wrapped in a crinkly plastic tablecloth). My ankle and knee were stiff and aching after a night on the dirt, so Logan had to help me to stand and tiptoe away from the nest of sleeping crew members.

"Where are we going?" I whispered.

He just smiled. "You'll find out."

We crossed the dirt road and walked through a stand of trees until we came to a clearing that looked out over the hills and flatlands below.

"What are we—" I began.

"Shh," he said again. "Just wait."

Logan spread a tablecloth on the ground for us to sit on, and we wrapped another one around our shoulders. "Look," he said, pointing.

Along the horizon, the tiniest blush of rose was just starting to lighten the deep purple sky.

My stomach did a complete flip.

"We're going to watch the sunrise," I whispered.

"I promised you we would."

"I thought you forgot."

He slipped an arm around my shoulders and stared out at the black line of the horizon. "I'm sorry I messed up that first morning. I got up late. And then when I heard you outside talking to Riley . . ."

"It's okay," I assured him. "This is perfect."

We didn't speak again as the sun began its show. The edge of the world grew brighter, and the sun threw pink streaks across the sky. All around us, the peaks of the mountains faded from gray to coral. And then the horizon became a streak of fiery orange and gold, spreading wide and then centering again in a sliver of molten light. Slowly, steadily, the sliver grew bigger, rounder, sharper, brighter, until it lit our faces and we had to squint and turn away from the glare.

And that's when it happened.

Logan and I both turned our heads at the same time. Toward each other. Our foreheads bumped. Then our noses. And then softly, shyly, our lips.

It was just a little kiss. Barely more than a whisper. But my insides felt liquid, molten, just like the sun we'd just watched. And I learned once again the proper use for the word *breathtaking*.

When we walked back to the camp, everyone else was starting to get up. By the looks of things, they were as tired and cold and stiff as I had been before the sunrise.

Liz had been digging around in the jeep and poked her head out when she heard Logan and me. "Good," she said. "You're up." She held out a couple packets of wet wipes and a bottle of water to each of us. "Here you go. Get yourselves cleaned up. We have an episode to shoot."

My heart dropped. I didn't want to go back to the same routine so soon. Like nothing had changed. I wasn't ready to give up the magic of that morning. Once we started in on the regular stuff, our moment on the hill would be over.

Logan eyed the (very cold) water bottle in his hand. "You're kidding, right?"

She gave him a stony look. "I never kid about the mini-sodes."

Deena did our makeup and braided back my hair while Ty strapped icy transmitters to our backs so he could wire us for our mics. I stood shivering, wishing the sun would hurry and warm things up already. It was just starting to peek up over the trees by then, so I guessed it was maybe about 10:30 or so. Another hour and a half and it would be straight overhead. Maybe then we'd get some heat.

When Deena and Ty finished with us, Liz instructed Logan and me on how we were going to tell the "people at home" about our breakdown dilemma. She had just gotten through explaining how she wanted us to remember to smile even though we were cold and dirty and tired and generally miserable, when Ty marched over to us and shoved his camera at her.

"Busted," he said.

The camera made a glassy rattling sound as she took it from him. "How on earth?"

"Don't know," Ty said. "Looks like it's been dropped. Or thrown. The insides are scrambled. It's completely worthless."

Liz's face went white. "And all the footage?"

"Saved on the memory card. But there'll be no more shooting. This thing is done. Kaput."

"Maybe you can use some of Bayani's equipment," Liz suggested.

"Good idea," Ty said. "If only Bayani were here. He's off at the other camp, and all his equipment is with him."

"Oh. Well." For the first time since I'd met her, Liz looked lost. "We'll figure something out," she said, and then wandered away.

Apparently released, Logan and I went looking for Becca and Riley. We found them by the barbecue grill, going through the boxes of food with Malo to see what they could make for breakfast. All the breakfast-y food must have gone with the other group, because none of them looked happy.

"What are we going to eat?" Riley asked.

"We could dig up some witchetty grubs," Malo offered. "Good bush tucker."

"What's a witchetty grub?" Logan asked.

Becca shuddered. "Don't ask."

"White," Riley said. "Slimy. Sluggy. Some folks put 'em on the barbie, but—"

"Bugs?" I caught Becca's shudder.

"Let's go look through those boxes again," Logan suggested.

"Any more clues this morning who's been . . . you know?" Becca asked quietly.

Riley shrugged. "Didn't see anything unusual last night. Nothing that would give anyone away, anyhow."

"But the perp must be here," Logan said. "Someone messed up Ty's camera since last night."

"I told you it wasn't anyone at home," Riley said.

"So who do you think it could—"

Becca was cut off by a loud "coo-ee." We turned to see Mr. Calder and Cavin, along with Mom and Dad and Bayani, trudging down the road toward us.

"Da!" Logan called, waving.

We ran over to them, and we weren't alone. Everyone crowded around them, firing questions, lodging complaints.

"Hold on, hold on," Cavin said wearily. "One at a time."

As I suspected, their jeep had been sabotaged, too. They didn't realize it until they had finished shooting Mom and Dad's segment and returned to the base camp. When they saw that the rest of us weren't there, Mr. Calder was going to hop in the jeep to look for us. That's when they discovered it wouldn't start, and then they started to get worried.

"We would have come back to you last night," Mom told me, "but all the flashlights were in one of the other jeeps and it was too dark."

"Malo coulda done it," Mr. Calder said, "but I ain't no tracker. Couldn't see enough to make it back."

"We left as soon as it got light," Dad added. Which meant they had been walking for several hours.

After everyone was caught up and fed (Malo had managed to pull together a breakfast of sausages, bread, and fruit), Mr. Calder offered to walk into town to get help.

"I'll come with you," Malo said, picking up his walking stick.

"Good on ya," Mr. Calder said. "Figured you would." Then to Riley and Becca he promised, "We'll be back before dark."

"And if you're not?" Becca asked, her voice straining.

"We will be." Mr. Calder kissed the top of her head and chucked Riley on the cheek, and then they were off.

Logan didn't waste any time gathering the four of us together as soon as Malo and Mr. Calder were out of sight.

"That gives us the day to figure out who's causing all the trouble," he said.

"In a controlled environment," Becca agreed. "It'll be like watching bugs under glass. Pretty soon someone will do something to give themselves away."

"Okay," I said. "Everyone split up. Let's mingle with everyone. Watch and listen. If you see anything, signal the rest of us."

"But act natural," Logan added.

Which was kind of funny, because we were all in the most unnatural situation ever. And no one was acting like themselves. By late afternoon, I was starting to get discouraged. If we didn't do something to shake up the "controlled environment" Becca had talked about, we were never going to solve the sabotage mystery.

I signaled everyone to meet behind the jeep again, and they did, quickly. Becca's face was flushed with excitement.

"What did you see? Who is it?"

"I don't know," I said. "They're all acting weird. Even Victoria."

"So what are we going to do?" Riley asked.

"We could gather everyone together so we can watch how they act with each other," Logan suggested. "Maybe play games while we're waiting for your dad and Malo."

"Not games," I said quickly. "You saw how Daniel got with charades. The idea is to bring them together, not push them apart."

"What do you suggest, then?" Becca asked. Not challenging, like she usually would be, but genuinely looking for an answer.

"How about songs around the campfire?"

Riley shook his head. "No campfire. Fire hazard."

"We could build a fire pit," Becca said. "It's permissible."

"Yeah," Logan said, "but you haven't heard my da sing."

"Okay," I said. "What about stories? Do you guys know the Dreamtime stories Malo is always talking about?"

"But the idea is to get everyone sharing, right?" Logan asked. "So everyone's got to tell something."

"Maybe instead of stories, we could talk about favorite books and movies, that sort of thing," Becca suggested.

"Not movies," Riley said. "Daniel's got a thing about Deena's movie connection."

"Okay." I ticked the limitations off on my fingers. "Not songs, not stories, no movies."

"What if we just ask everyone what they miss most, being stuck out here in the bush?" Riley asked.

"That's easy," Logan said. "Food."

But at the same time, I said, "Hot water," and Becca said, "Texting."

"You see?" Riley said. "Good conversation starter."

"All right." Logan looked back toward the camp. "Now all we have to do is to get everyone together."

Turns out that wasn't as hard as we might have thought. Hunger is a good motivator. Riley and Becca showed everyone how to make "damper," which is a biscuit-type bread traditionally cooked right on the coals in the outback. They were kind enough to cover the coals with foil before cooking our samples, though. Early Australian settlers used to practically live on damper, Riley said, and drovers still made it all the time.

Liz, of course, had both of them wired so we could at least record them. She set Ty about taking still shots to go with their demonstration.

Victoria boiled hot water for tea on another part of the fire, and everyone seemed happy enough to sit around the fire pit, "taking" their tea (as Victoria would say) and sampling hot damper. Ty even set down the camera and joined in, which was exactly what we wanted.

When everyone was about done, Logan stared into the fire and said longingly, "You know what I miss most about now? Playing a little footie." That's what Logan called European football, or soccer.

"Or cricket," Riley said.

They both should have won awards for their acting skills. You've never seen two such sad-looking boys in one place. Or maybe they were serious, I don't know. The important thing is it got everyone commiserating.

"How about a long, hot shower?" Deena said.

Mom nodded. "Or a clean kitchen to cook in."

It was perfect. Everyone started talking about things they missed, and what was the first thing they would do when we got back. Except it didn't tell me anything. Everyone was participating. Laughing. Looking very un-guilty. So much for revealing the guilty party.

The fire started to die down, and I worried that the group would break up once there were no more flames in the pit to mesmerize them.

"I'm going to grab some more wood," I said, standing.

"You sit tight," Jack said. "I can do it."

He got up from his chair and lumbered into the woods behind us. I settled back down and kept watching everyone. Especially Ty and Deena. I really didn't want Deena to be the bad guy, so I kept waiting for Ty to give some kind of hint that it was him. Only he seemed so nice and genuine. But he and Deena were the newest crew members. Everyone else had been with us long enough to have loyalty to the show. I hoped.

Then I looked back at the fire. Weak little licks of fire darted up around glowing embers, but that was it. Where was Jack with the wood? I looked toward the trees impatiently, waiting for him to appear with an armful, but I didn't see him.

"I'm going to go see if I can help Jack," I told Logan. He started to get up, but I signaled for him to stay where he was and to watch everyone while I was gone. I think he got the message, because he settled back onto his seat and gave me a little nod. I left the scrutiny to him and followed Jack's path into the woods.

I didn't see him anywhere. But I did see lots of brush and deadwood he could have picked up to bring back to the fire. Where had he gone? Maybe he knew where to find bigger pieces of wood. "Jack?" I called. No answer. I kept walking.

It didn't take more than a few minutes before I started to get nervous. After my adventure in the woods the night before, I was more than a little afraid of getting lost again. What if that's what happened to Jack?

I called out "Coo-ee!" When I got no answer, I glanced

back toward the camp (which, of course, I couldn't see through the trees by then), wondering if maybe I should go back and get help.

Then I thought I heard a voice. Not calling back, but talking. I walked toward the sound. Soon I could hear enough to know it wasn't Jack. I froze. Who could it be? Malo and Mr. Calder had gone to find help. Everyone else was sitting round the fire pit. And where was Jack?

I crept closer to the voice, wincing each time my toe hit a rock or a twig snapped beneath my foot. For all I knew, the voice could be help. But I'd been looking for a saboteur all afternoon, and that tends to make you wary. I wanted to see whoever it was before that person saw me.

And then I heard the voice say, "Listen, I've done my job. More than my job, actually. Camping out in the bush was never part of the deal."

Whoever it was stood just ahead, holding a long, boxy thing up to his ear. A phone? I thought we were in a dead zone.

He began to pace, and I was able to get a clearer view of him. The recognition hit me with a physical force that made me take a step back. It was the Camera Guy from back at the ranch.

"Yeah, well, they've only got one more day and then—" The person on the other end of the line must have said something Camera Guy didn't like because he flapped his free arm like a sick buzzard. "No, you listen to me. I did it. The show is finished. Now you just keep your end of the bargain."

The show? Finished? Suddenly, I felt as if I had swallowed one of those witchetty grubs Riley and Becca had been talking about. All those times I saw Camera Guy watching us, watching the crew . . . all those times I thought he was just a silly tourist . . . he'd been scheming.

I had to tell Logan. And Riley and Becca. And my mom and dad. Watching him through the tree branches, I started to back up. Not as quietly as I had come, apparently, because his head whipped around, and he peered into the woods in my direction. I froze.

"Gotta go," he said to whoever was on the other end of the line. "I'll check in later." Stabbing a grubby finger at the phone to end his call, he marched into the trees, just to the left of where I was standing. I closed my eyes as the relief flooded over me. So he hadn't seen me, then. Now all I had to do was to get out of there before he did.

Holding my breath, I took another careful step backward. And another, then I turned to run back to the camp.

And ran straight into Camera Guy.

C 21

Camera Guy stared down at me, and I raised my chin to stare back. "Who are you?" I demanded with a whole lot more confidence than I felt. Inside, I was whimpering. But I couldn't let him see that.

He ignored my question. "You're a lot dumber that you look," he told me. "Didn't you learn your lesson about wandering around in the woods when you got yourself lost last night?"

He may as well have just punched me in the stomach. I could accept the fact that he'd been watching us for days, but the idea that he may have been in the woods the whole time I was lost sent new shivers slithering down my spine. And here we were again. Only this time, I had seen him. This time I was cornered. Alone. Helpless.

Or maybe not. Somewhere in the trees, Jack was gathering firewood. I had to keep this guy talking . . . loudly enough that Jack could hear and come find us.

"Who were you talking to?" I raised my voice just a bit—but not so much that he would become suspicious. I hoped.

"None of your business," he snapped.

"How'd you even get a call out?" I asked, even louder this time.

"Satellite phone," he told me.

Come on. Come on. Where was Jack? I raised my voice even louder. "What did you mean just now when you said you had done your part? What did you do?"

He laughed, but it wasn't a happy sound. "You're a smart girl," he said. "You figure it out."

"You've been trying to turn the crew against each other," I said.

"Not trying to," he said with a sneer. "Did."

"But why?"

"Moola. Dinero. Greenbacks," he said. "It was a paying gig. You'd be surprised how much money matters."

"You'd be surprised how much it doesn't," Malo said.

Camera Guy clenched his hands and spun around to take a swing, but he was too slow. Malo grabbed the man's fist and twisted his hand backward, forcing him to his knees. "You have a lot of explaining to do."

● ● ● ● ●

Malo and Mr. Calder had arrived at camp just after I left the campfire, it seems. When Logan told Malo I had gone into the woods after Jack, Malo came looking for me. Probably remembering how lost I had gotten myself the night before.

What he found instead was Jack, on the ground, groaning and holding his head. Jack told Malo how he had come across Camera Guy, watching the camp through the trees. The last thing Jack remembered, he had tried to confront the guy and ended up getting whacked on the head with a piece of the very wood he had gone into the woods to gather. Malo made sure Jack was going to be all right, and then he came after me.

"Good thinking to keep him talking," he told me, "I was able to follow your voice right to you." And to Camera Guy he said, "You're coming with me."

The guy just laughed. "I don't think so, old man. I saw you last night. You couldn't even lift that little girl to carry her out of the woods. You think you're going to overpower me?"

Malo held his stock whip in front of Camera Guy's face. "You'll be coming with us unless you'd rather feel the crack of the whip."

Camera Guy's eyes widened for a moment, and then he bowed his head like he was beaten, but as soon as Malo started to put the whip away, the guy lunged at him. He grabbed Malo around the legs and tackled him to the ground.

I didn't mean to, but I screamed. Like that would help.

Camera Guy scrabbled to grab hold of Malo's whip, clawing Malo in the process. That was more than I could take. I jumped into the tangle of arms and legs, pounding his wide back, pulling on his hands, yelling for him to let go.

It didn't take much for him to toss me aside. Just one sweep of his arm and I was down on the ground, fresh pain searing through my hurt knee.

"Give it up, old man," Camera Guy said through his teeth. "I'm leaving, and there's nothing you can do to stop me."

"Not so fast," a voice said.

It was my dad. And Bayani. And Jack. And Ty. And Logan. And then everyone else. They rushed to Malo's aid and pulled Camera Guy off of him. Riley stretched out his hand to help me up.

"Nice work, Hollywood," he said.

Back at camp, Camera Guy confessed everything. He used to work for the network before he got canned (why, he wouldn't tell us). He was low on money and high on resentment when an agent for *A Foreign Affair* approached him with a plan to ruin the Australia shoot. "They didn't care how I did it," he said. "As long as I managed to keep it going long enough to shut you down."

"And you figured the best way to do that was to create a rift within the crew," Dad said, catching on.

Camera Guy laughed his joyless laugh again. "Oh, yeah. Messed-up equipment you can replace. Makeup you can get along without. But pull apart the team . . ."

Daniel's face went completely white as he listened to the confession. Probably because he realized how well he had played into Camera Guy's plans. "How? How could you know what would pull us apart?"

Camera Guy sneered. "You know what? I asked myself the same thing when I first took the job. How could I mess with the group enough to throw off an entire shoot? But then I saw how jealous you were of Pinky here"—he pointed to Deena—"and it hit me. I knew exactly what to do. So thanks for that, man. Envy is a powerful thing."

The ride back down to the property was a somber one. At least in our jeep. Deena kept staring out the window and dabbing at her eyes. Ty muttered to himself about how we had all been played. Liz shook her head and *tsked* about how easy it had been to turn the team against one another. Like a pack of wild dogs is how she put it.

At least they had an excuse. I had managed to get jealous all on my own and had almost ruined the trip to Australia because of it. I looked to Logan and sighed. What idiots we'd been. He smiled at me like he knew what I was thinking and took my hand. As my fingers curled around his, I made a promise to myself never to let anything as petty as jealousy come between Logan and me ever again.

The police had arrived at our "camp" about the same time as our mechanic. Mr. Calder had been able to summon them with Camera Guy's own satellite phone. While the first handcuffed Camera Guy and helped him into the back of their yellow-and-blue-checkered fourby, the second started by replacing the serpentine belt on the jeep.

"Bit of an adventure, I hear," Mrs. Calder said as we all piled out of the fourbies. "You get yourself cleaned up, and I'll get started on the tucker. Liz, I've shown your guests to the stables so they could get the lay of the land. I wasn't sure when you would be back, so I suggested they see what's available so they could set up their shots and then—"

Liz shook her head. "The photographers are here *today*?" She dug in her bag for her tablet and waited for it to boot up. "The magazine people weren't supposed to come until tomorrow," she mumbled. "I'm sure of it."

"They said someone called and rescheduled for this evening," Mrs. Calder said.

Logan and I looked at each other. "Camera Guy," we said together.

"Well, if they've come all the way up, ye'll just have to make the best of it," Cavin said.

"Timing's good," Ty offered. "The natural light early evening is perfect for stills. But you'd better hurry. Sun's already hanging low."

"I need to shower first," I said, gesturing to my dirty clothes and bandaged knee.

"Well, do it quickly," Liz ordered me. "Deena can do an expedited job on your hair and makeup."

Deena looked dazed, but she nodded. "I'll try."

"I can help," Daniel offered.

Startled, Deena looked up at him. I could see in her eyes that she wanted to accept his offer, but she was still unsure. But after a moment's hesitation, she smiled at him and said, "Thanks. I'd appreciate that."

I should have known the photographer would be more interested in Logan than she was in me. A couple of days ago, it would have bothered me. Now I thought it was funny.

We were shooting for a girls' magazine, after all. And that required a lot of wardrobe changes. Suddenly, Logan was the darling of our designer sponsors. They knew their demographic. The girls who read the magazine might want to see the outfits I was wearing, but they most definitely would want to *look* at Logan.

Some of the shots we did together, but many of them featured Logan up front while I was positioned somewhere in the background. Then the photographer asked me to step aside for a moment so she could get shots of Logan alone. Logan gave me a sheepish smile and a shrug, and I just smiled. I could just imagine the flurry of questions I'd be getting for the next Ask Cass session.

Victoria stood by me as we watched Logan pose for

the camera. "What's the male equivalent of *la chica moda*?" I asked.

"I'm not sure," she said. "Perhaps *el hombre moda*?"

I laughed. "That's perfect. I'm going to start calling him *hombre* for short."

I didn't realize Riley and Becca had come to watch until I heard Becca laugh. "He doesn't look like an *hombre* to me. More like a *guapo*."

Victoria smiled. "'Handsome,' hmm?"

Becca blushed. I should have known. Becca was a groupie, too, even though Logan was younger than she was.

"*Guapo*," I repeated. I liked it.

I tried the new name out on Logan that evening after dinner. He just rolled his eyes and laughed.

"So you're okay with it?" I asked him.

"I'm okay with whatever you want to call me," he said, "as long as you call me."

"Like, on the phone?" I asked. I was so confused.

He laughed again. "I meant talk to me, but sure. You can call me on the phone. Texting's good, too."

We sat on a bench under one of the eucalyptus trees and watched the crew as they left the dining hall. Joking with each other. Being silly. Laughing.

"It's so good to have everything back to normal," I said.

He nodded and slipped his arm around me. "It really

is," he said. "I didn't like us being mad at each other like before."

"Me either," I said. "I'm really sorry about—"

"It's over," Logan said. "I'm sorry, too. Let's just promise not to go there again."

"Deal."

"Deal," he repeated.

He smiled and I melted a little inside. I could see why he had so many groupies. And now, like Malo said, I was happy for his success. It felt a whole lot better than being jealous.

And besides, those other girls could dream about him all they wanted. He was *my* best friend. I knew that now. I didn't have to spell out anything. I didn't have to tell him how much I liked him. Anyone who could still want to be with me after the week we'd had was the kind of friend who didn't need explanations.

Logan nudged me closer. "I like Australia," he said.

I leaned my head on his shoulder. "So do I," I told him. "So do I."

I thought Dad would be happy when he got the news. Not turn-cartwheels-in-the-living-room happy, but I figured he might at least smile. Instead, tension strained between his brows as he read the e-mail, and the corners of his mouth tugged downward.

"What is it?" I asked.

He didn't seem to hear me, but pushed back in his chair and hollered for my mom. "Julia! Come take a look at this!"

Dad and Gramma and I had been sitting at the breakfast table in Gramma's kitchen, waiting for Mom to join us so we could eat. Dad pulled out his phone and was checking e-mails when he suddenly froze. I looked to Gramma and she shrugged, but a worry crease deepened in her forehead.

Mom's slippers whispered across the old linoleum floor

as she padded into the kitchen, still buttoning the cuffs on her blouse. "My goodness, what is it that can't wait until—" He held his phone out to her and she leaned down to read what was on the screen. "Oh."

"What is it?" I asked again, raising my voice a little in case Mom was suffering from the same selective hearing as Dad.

"It's *A Foreign Affair*," Mom said. "The show has been canceled."

Was that all? We'd known for weeks that they were in trouble. Even though everyone at *A Foreign Affair* had denied ever having met the Camera Guy, let alone having paid him to sabotage our show, two confessions by two people in the space of three months was enough to make the authorities take a second look. The *Foreign Affair* producer tried to downplay the investigation to the media, but it was a scandal that was just too juicy to go away.

Cavin always said no publicity was bad publicity, but *A Foreign Affair*'s ratings tanked. The tabloids and gossip shows said the makers of *A Foreign Affair* had been jealous of *When in Rome*'s market share, and that's why they went after us the way they did. Viewers apparently didn't think it was cool for one show to try to destroy another in such a way, so a whole bunch of them stopped watching *A Foreign Affair*. Now their network had decided not to renew the show's contract.

"But that's a good thing, right?" I asked. "Less competition and all?" Plus, now *A Foreign Affair* wouldn't be around to pay people to mess with our show. I couldn't see how that could be bad.

Mom pulled out her chair and sat down. "It's always a shame to see a good show leave the air."

Dad turned off his phone and returned it to his pocket. "A little friendly competition is a good thing," he told me. "It pushes you to try harder. To do better. Besides, if other shows do well, it keeps viewers interested in travel and culture, and that can only be good for us."

"A rising tide lifts all boats," Gramma agreed.

How sad the people at *A Foreign Affair* didn't see that. I never watched it, but Mom said it was a good show. It had to be if it was our main rival (if I don't say so myself). And now, they lost their viewers, they lost their credibility, and they lost their show.

And all because they couldn't put down the dingo.

Logan wrote the final blog entry for Australia, but he wouldn't let me see it before he sent it in. It took some adjustment for me to get used to sharing the blog, but I wasn't jealous about it anymore. After our sunrise (and kiss!), Logan and I have a new sort of connection. It seems fitting that he should share in reporting the best moments of our time together.

It's up, he texted me when the feed went live. **Network approved and posted.**

I rushed to my computer and logged onto the network website, drumming my fingers impatiently until I could pull up the blog.

They asked me to guest post on Cass's blog to tell you about our time in Australia. I'm not much of a blogger, so I'll just give you my list of the top ten reasons to visit Australia.

10.   It's cool.

9.   It's pretty.

8.   The people are awesome.

7.   The swimming's great.

6.   Brumbies.

5.   The outback.

4.   The tucker.

3.   The Back of Beyond.

2.   Good friends.

1.   The best sunrises in the entire world.

Catch all the action!

Get Hooked
ON THESE OTHER
FABULOUS
Girl Series!

Lucy B. Parker: Girl vs. Superstar
By Robin Palmer

Forever Four
By Elizabeth Cody Kimmel

Lights, Camera, Cassidy: Episode 1: Celebrity
By Linda Gerber

Almost Identical
By Lin Oliver

Check out sample chapters at
http://tinyurl.com/penguingirlsampler